A thread finer than spider web
bonds me to this majestic,
lightning bolt beauty.
Why is it me who was chosen?
Or, did I choose, choose my Self,
to be the one to pull reality out of space
and expose it on earth.

Dedication

In memory of my beloved grandparents,
William Luke Lawlor
and
Anne Louise Moore Lawlor

Thank you for always loving me the most.

Acknowledgements

First and foremost I thank my best friend, Tommy Garbellotto, for all of his help and support during the publication of this book. I would like to thank my mother, Ann Law, for accompanying me to the United Kingdom to do research. And for lending me the house at Grace's Cove, in the winter of 2002, where I wrote *Segment One: Sage.* I would also like to gratefully acknowledge all of the ladies of the Block Island Library, Lonni, Amy, Kristin, Bonny, and Pam, for being so helpful during that same winter when I had all of my questions regarding research and computers. Also of Block Island I thank Diana Adams for her invaluable assistance with Microsoft Word, and Bernice Johnson for the Scooby snacks. Of the Nantucket Atheneum, I would like to thank Lincoln and Paula for all of their help in the spring of 2001 when I wrote the first four chapters of *Sage*. Also of Nantucket, I thank Elizabeth Hughes, Melanie Wernick, Melissa Dudley, Roy Weedon, and John McGrath for reading *Segment One: Sage* and for your tremendous support and feedback. And to my dear old housemate and friend, Ethan McMorrow, thank you for getting me from floppy to CD that winter we lived on Pond Road.

There are more people on Nantucket than I could ever name who, patiently year after year, were supportive about this book. You know who you are; please know that your unwavering belief formed a foundation that helped bring this book to the point of publication. Of all people, Jordan Ferreira asked me the most, "So how's it going with your book?"

Thank you to all of the people who tilted their heads sideways and asked, "Is it fiction?" after I told them the book was about a magician who brings a lost world back into reality. That was my favorite question, and it gave me infinite support to keep going.

To Tom Congdon, senior editor of Doubleday Books (and editor of Peter Benchley's *JAWS*), I thank you for your professional opinion and praise. And without question, I thank Suse Robinson (of Nantucket) for connecting me with

Mr. Congdon. I also thank my brother, Roark Loedy, for his inspiration and enthusiasm.

I wish to thank all members of The Grateful Dead, alive and dead, for inspiring me with my favorite music; and especially for the New Years '78 jam from *Dark Star* into *The Other One*: this single piece of music has inspired me my whole life, and especially did so during the writing of this book. Also thanks to the Jerry Garcia Band for the 2/29/80 *Midnight Moonlight*.

To my dearest friends: Silver, Tommy Garbellotto, Melissa Russo, Tim Barca, Kara Williams, Ania Camplin, Brooke Bedell, Cary Thrash, Robin Gibson, Laura Maurer, Glenn Spitz, Steve Dober, Dennis McCarthy, Brad Phelps, Barry Donovan, Gregg Nosiglia, and Elizabeth (Bizzer) Wykoff: I love you all, and thank you from the depths of my heart for always being there for me.

The arcane cover border is a magic spell which I wrote, and translated into the Runic. I did the lettering myself. If you want to decipher it, all you need is the Runic alphabet and some patience. It begins in the lower left corner.

Contents

Enter.

This book is a gateway. You become part of the magic occurrence by reading it. This is a dream. You've been admitted; the price is to leave your mind at the door. By reading this book, you become part of this dream.

There is a memory stored in the depths of your mind. The part of the human psyche that remembers magic is becoming unveiled and enlarged. The part of the human psyche that stores Avalon is awakening. That's what this book is about.

It is the inhibition of magic that is the cause of all suffering. It is time to drop down to a deeper level, to tap in to the magic vein. We all live within the very matrix of magic, that core where magic originates: where you are a vortex of power, a spiraling helix of blood and water and twisted stairways of DNA. Where lightning is God's blood, and thunder is God's voice.

> I am the gateway. You are the gateway.
> To reach a masterpiece, to reach a
> pinnacle, a summit,
> enter ancientness and high times.
> Enter the veins of lightning.
> Ascend to your destiny:
> Live free or die.

Segment One:
Sage

One

THE CARDS OF THE CHALICE

Sweet, pale green molecules of spring air permeated the dense British forest. The spirits of the ancient trees wove amongst the trunks. They had a human visitor. She was strong, with rugged legs. She was beautiful in rather an eerie, otherworldly sort of way, with green slanted cat eyes and blondish brown hair. This woman—girl—was only sixteen years old. But she was wise beyond her years. Maybe she had just grown into her name: Sage. Or maybe she was just born wise. So the spirits of the ancient trees let her stay.

The human visitor approached the small stream which was hidden in the forest's depths. She was remembering why she was here. Memories of the preceding evening flooded her mind. The man's fist came down upon the dinner table, so hard it caused the earthenware crock to shatter, and the food it had taken her mother two hours to make flew about the room, even hitting the walls. Sage, her mother, and her two little brothers shrank back from the tyrant that was her father. He had flown into another of his daily rages. He slapped one brother sideways across the head, causing him to fall to the floor. The other brother hid behind a chair with a white face, food stuck to his clothing. All that was audible after the crock had shattered were violent loud curses and threats, some curses not even in British but from other lands. Each of her father's curses was like a dagger, and he threw them while glowering into their eyes—and he would not allow them to look away. He threw his dagger-like curses directly into their eye sockets, where the torture could live as memory.

Sage advanced to her favorite rock by the stream that she usually sat on to ponder. The stream was edged with many rocks and plentiful moss, which was emerald green and as thick as fur. Sage thought of the moss as magical. She knew that being around moss, feeling its soft texture, and most especially walking on it with bare feet were all experiences that soothed her and brought peace to her heart. To get away from home,

Sage had already been using the forest as her cocoon for years. She felt a presence with her extra sensory perception, and looked up to see the Lynx. He had become her best friend in the last few years. She was very lucky to have been befriended by a Lynx. It did not matter that the Lynx was not human and therefore did not speak her language. Actually she preferred it. She far preferred all of his different purring and growling sounds to the sound of humans speaking her own language.

As soon as they locked eyes he made a specialized cat sound: a trilling, high purring meow. He came and rubbed against her leg and she stroked him. He had a large, pronounced muzzle and big furry tufts at the tops of his ears. He had an ivory ruff around his neck, and a thick, bushy, grayish-tan coat, lightly speckled with spots. Each of his paws was the size of a bear's. Sage looked into the Lynx's gold eyes. Looking in those eyes was looking into magic, healing, soothingness and the truth. This Lynx gave to her a sense of family, almost as if she were a cat herself. His gold eyes were so deep; he seemed more of a person than any human she had ever met. Plus, she had always loved cats. To be around such a big cat and not have to be scared was a great blessing.

She knew enough of being scared in her own home. Sage knew instinctively that it wasn't right that she should have to live in a constant state of fear. She decided that nothing was worth going back to the dwelling of that horrid rageful man. She thought: *He's not a man and never will be.* She tried not to think of how much he had tortured her. She decided that enduring his acute cruelty had made her the incredibly strong girl she knew she was. It was the only way she could accept the way she had been treated. But she resolved in her heart to someday rescue her mother and brothers.

This morning there was something unusual, not befitting the stream bed. There was something on her sitting rock. It was a hand woven pouch with a neck strap. The pouch was woven of multicolored yarns, red, orange, pink, and blue; the yarns woven into diamond shapes. The bottom of the pouch was decorated with three bright, tassel-like balls, one green, one pink, and one orange. Of all the rocks upon the stream bed, the pouch had been placed upon her rock; so she knew the offering was for her.

It seemed almost like the pouch was quivering in her hands as she opened the flap, as if something was alive in there. She pulled out a deck of thick, ornate cards. Each had a picture that genuinely looked three dimensional. The backside of each card was purple and had a lightning bolt with a cat's paw print stamped across it. She glanced into one picture, and could not stop staring— because it looked like a true living landscape—as if she could shrink herself and enter. A miniature winding path leading into a stand of trees curved just so, and the trees moved in wind inaudible to her.

Artos waited a while before approaching Sage. It was to be his first time meeting her, and he did not want to startle her. He was a soothsayer; a wiseman who lived in the main forest. He knew the Lynx too. It was Artos who decided that Sage was meant to have those cards. It was her destiny, and he knew it. He knew about the tremendously mossy place by the stream where Sage liked to sit, and he knew that she often came there shortly after sunrise. Upon that large, flat rock that was her usual seat, Artos had placed the pouch. So as not to surprise her, he made a good bit of noise upon approaching, like a deer that does not yet sense danger. Sage looked up to see the deer which instead was a man. Artos: he was dressed in greens, grays and browns, which made him camouflaged in the forest. His long silver hair blended with the sky, and his eyes were blue.

"Greetings to you, My Lady." He bowed, and somehow his voice sounded like a harp.

"And to you as well, Sir." Her own voice was low and deep for a young woman.

"What brings you into the forest?"

"This is my usual place." Sage noticed that she felt safe and comfortable conversing with him, even though she was alone in the woods and she was a young girl and he was a man. It was a good feeling.

"I am Artos. And your name?"

"Sage. Sage Uberchat."

"Uberchat. Interesting. Familiar are you with the study of languages?"

Sage waited. Why was he asking her this?

"Sir, I am unfamiliar. Why do you ask?"

Artos breathed in deeply. "Uber means super in German. And chat means cat in French. Of course it depends a bit on how your name is spelled. But I find it interesting that, to me, it sounds like your surname means 'Supercat.' "

Supercat. Sage thought about this.

"High quality. Above the rest." Artos breathed. "And of course," he smiled a little as he gestured toward the Lynx, "here is the cat."

Sage took note of the fact that she did not feel intruded upon by this man. Artos must know the Lynx, she thought. She could tell by the way the cat was rubbing his furry cheek against Artos's leg. "So you're telling me I'm a Super Cat?" She almost giggled. It was unlike her to make jokes. For her this was an attempt at humor, which indicated how comfortable she felt around Artos and the Lynx.

Artos laughed. "Your father must have had French and German ancestry which combined enough at one point to have created such an unusual, and superb, name."

She never had thought of Uberchat as being superb, though she had always liked it. Artos spoke again. "Now then, my lady. You have a fascinating pouch."

Sage trusted Artos before she mentally realized it. Which led her to blurt: "Yes sir, I have just found it! It is a gift for me, I know it is! I know so because, when I arrived here, this pouch was right on my rock." She said "my" with distinct ownership; indeed, the rock itself had grown accustomed to her vibrations.

"What's in the pouch?" Artos asked naturally.

"Sir it is filled with great cards!" At this, all of Sage's attention funneled back into the cards. She realized that she had temporarily forgotten them upon the arrival of Artos. Now she resumed her mesmerization. "They are stunningly beautiful—look." She held the whole stack, about two inches thick, out to him. Artos accepted the cards, touched to his soul that Sage, the young innocent girl, already trusted him so deeply. *So lucky that I am trustworthy,* he thought.

Since the cards were always changing, and so exquisite, it was easy for Artos to feign astonishment. He had never taken these cards for granted. "You are a blessed girl, to have been chosen to be the holder of these cards. For these are the Cards of the Chalice."

The leaves seemed not to move, for a moment. The stream for an instant seemed to stop its flow. There was an abatement of wind, and even the Lynx did not breathe. It was one of those moments where everything stopped, because only one thing could be heard over and over again in Sage's mind: *These are the Cards of the Chalice.* Over and over again. It was a chant, a mantra.

"What does that mean?" she asked in awe.

Artos by now had chosen his own sitting rock and was lowering himself onto it as Sage asked this question. He spoke. "In Avalon there was a well. It had the finest water, and the priestesses of the Goddess could drink only this. Chalice Well, it was called. One day my distant relative, who was a priestess, was alone by the well, staring into its waters. She became startled because a card, one of these cards, floated to the surface and hovered there till she took it. You see, Sage, magic reigned in the past, especially in Avalon.

"One after another, the cards emerged from the well water. My relative was the receiver of this full deck of cards. She was so in awe, she stacked them neatly, all upright, and waited, barely even looking at their pictures, because it was just too much to bear. And she said later that it was the only time the Goddess spoke inside of her mind. 'Selchie.' (That was her name). 'Selchie. These are the Cards of the Chalice. They hold secrets of the future of Avalon. You can not yet know from where they come, but you are responsible for where they go. It is someone's destiny to receive them. It is for you to pass them along with wisdom and discernment, until they reach their true owner.' "

Comprehension began dawning in Sage's mind. "You mean—you—have given me these cards?!"

Artos looked at her kindly. "Only in the most basic sense. They have been passed along in my family for centuries, waiting for their true owner. I now pass them on to you, but the discernment comes from deep within my soul: that it is your Destiny to use them, and to discover the secrets of the future of Avalon."

Two

THE TREEHOUSE

A vast stillness was produced, as a result of his words. Her ESP was helping Sage now, for it unveiled a knowing that existed beyond her mind. A weaker person would have run from this responsibility. But Sage's newly accessed enlightenment became her, and she spoke: "I accept."

Again there was a great pause. The Lynx stared at Sage, and Artos watched the Lynx stare at her. *He will become her teacher,* Artos thought, of the Lynx. The moss vibrated its greenness, the stream water trickled over the rocks, and warm molecules from the sun infused the land. Sage's perfect, translucent face wore a new dignity, a new highness. The freshly enlightened part of her created a glow around her body. Sage could feel the thick, strong, cat vibrations from the Lynx as he sat beside her.

Artos' blue eyes were so riveting, they seemed to take over that entire section of forest, as if the whole forest were behind him, and he the guard of the Otherworld. It was to these eyes that Sage spoke, and she felt she was entering a much more real world than she had heretofore known. "Artos, I now have need to integrate all that has befallen on this morn. Let us meet two days hence. And we will discuss these Cards."

He nodded, the waves of his silver hair falling forward a bit. Then the blue eyes looked at her again: "Meet me at the fortress—you know the one—that seems abandoned, in semi-ruin?"

"At the fortress, then," said Sage, and she rose from the rock, gave Artos a small smile and vanished into the forest growth, the bright colors of the card pouch the last sight to disappear. The Lynx stayed behind with Artos.

In perhaps what was the space of one hour, Sage came upon her secret hiding place. The secret hiding place was, next to being befriended by the Lynx, one of her most lucky acquisitions. Someone had built a quite sturdy treehouse in a remote part of the forest. Upon discovering it many years earlier, Sage had spied on it for a full year before she decided it was abandoned, and safe for her use. A true craftsman must have built it. Oak was used, so it was very strong. Ivy wound around the ladder and up to the house. The tree in which it was built was huge with many limbs. The treehouse was big enough for Sage to comfortably lie down in, and it was wide enough to be like a tiny room. She had carried her basket, full of dry leaves, over and over again up the ladder, to make her bed. She spread an old, but clean and thick quilt over the leaves, for sleeping.

There were two small windows. They had glass (the very first glass) with bubbles and uneven thickness, so when she looked out, the world looked ripply, and bubbly, wavering and askew. The funny little windows were one of her favorite things about the treehouse. Her grandmother, her mother's mother, had taught her how to dry fruits, apples and pears, and these she had in jars in one corner of the treehouse. It was very pleasant in there, with her little bed and beautiful quilt from the same grandmother, and ivy growing inside through cracks. She had brought from home a blue bowl full of lavender, pussy willows, rose petals, and cat whiskers (collected from all her favorite cats). There were some dried flowers from last autumn, still giving off a little color. It truly was a place of peace, and Sage knew how lucky she was to have it. She had even brought in a small, round, three-legged stool for sitting, which she had lugged from a nearby town.

Sage was a good breather, always taking deep soothing breaths. She had found that it was the best way to relax, and most people never thought of it. They were quick to the brandy, the whisky. But those drinks made her feel bad. Breathing the fresh, pine-scented air of the forest made her feel healthy and strong, and she always had the clean clear water of the stream. So she sat on her little three-legged stool, in front of one of the windows. She breathed and stared outside. A stag flashed by, with a great rack of antlers. This was a good omen. Sage knew it was very rare for a stag to still have its antlers by springtime. Mostly Sage was wondering why Artos had given her the cards. He had said that it was her destiny to use them. Then she pondered about the fortress, which was in a state of semi-ruin. Sage had never been inside of it. She had briefly seen it from the outside, and knew roughly where it was. She was very much looking forward to going in there.

Sage began thinking of a boy she had loved. She still loved him, in fact. It wasn't even that long ago that she had last seen him. His name was Dane, and he was named after his father, who was a Viking warrior. Dane had blonde hair and blue eyes and was the most beautiful boy Sage had ever seen. Dane's father's massive pirate ship had been forced to anchor at the tiny port near Sage's family's town. They were in sore need of rations. It was not a time of plunder for them and they were only there for a fortnight collecting what foods they could.

At that time, Sage was often down by the docks staring at the sea and the boats, so she was watching for hours as the majestic Viking ship drew closer and closer. Seeing the huge white sails billowing in the wind was magnificent, and Sage was mesmerized. Sun on the water, wind in the sails, the great wooden ship drew closer, complete with a dragon-headed bow. The carved dragon's tongue was red. She watched the men load into the dinghy that would take them to the shore.

From her distance, she thought she had seen a shock of bright blonde hair, the bright blonde that only youth can carry. But it was upon their arrival on the sand that Sage saw him. Young Dane. He was older than she was, perhaps by a few years. Sage felt that feeling that she had to know him, to be near him. She wasn't just seeing his outer beauty, but that from within. Once they met, they had spent whole days together, as much time as possible until he had to return to the sea. She had fallen in love with him during that short time.

She snapped herself out of reverie. "That was months ago," she told herself. "Be present." She would think of Dane later. Now she had her destiny to consider. Sage hadn't given much thought to destiny before, but once Artos said it to her, it lit a flame in her heart. It pulled her into the future and made her feel that feeling of having a purpose in life. Sage deeply was enjoying this feeling, of having an important purpose and even a teacher to guide her. And the cards were so mysterious.

She glanced over at the card pouch as it lay on her bed, with its red, orange, pink and blue yarn diamonds. The pouch seemed to almost quiver. Slowly she picked it up and reached inside. Without looking, she chose one card. When she drew it out, and looked at it, she looked in on a landscape. There was water, a lake. Lots of trees surrounding the lake. And—a beaver. A beaver? There it was swimming around. Sage liked beavers and thought they were charming but did not expect to see one inside of a landscape on a divination card. It actually seemed that she could reach in and touch it with the tip of one finger. She refrained though, unsure.

What did the beaver mean? She would ask Artos. The beaver dove down and did not come back up so she slid the card gently back in with the rest of the deck, closed the pouch and placed it back on the bed. *This is good,* she thought. *I feel right about this.* Though full of relief at being away from her father, leaving home had been frightening. Now she felt the purpose in life feeling again and was grateful. For she could have a life of using these cards, to guide her and maybe even to help others. Leaving home felt less scary now.

A guttural purring growling sound issued from outside, down on the ground. Sage knew it was her Lynx. Opening the tiny door, she quietly called, "Come on in, Lynx." The cat bounded up, the ladder a cinch for him. In he came, all sixty pounds of thick furred wild feline. She stroked his fur with both of her hands, starting with his face and going all the way down his sides to his bobbed tail. The Lynx was very indulgent with her. She was the only human he had ever had contact with, except Artos. He loved her, as much as a wild cat can love.

Sage's favorite thing he did was purr. The purr of a Lynx is quite different than that of a domestic cat—it is about ten times louder and very rumbling and not unlike quiet thunder. Listening to the Lynx always made all Sage's problems melt away and disappear from her mind. Now she lay on the leaf bed with him, petting him while he purred her into tranquility. It was a cat lover's utopia.

"Lynx, do you want to come to the fortress with me tomorrow?" She always talked to him, not caring that he knew not what she said. But then, he always talked to her, in his way, and just the sounds from him soothed her. She hoped his experience was as fulfilling as hers. It must have been, or else he wouldn't have been there. It was not as if she was feeding him. Cats are funny, if they like someone, they will go to that person even if the person gives them nothing. The Lynx might not have known precisely what Sage was saying to him, but often he actually had somewhat of an idea, as was indicated by his behavior. This time, a slightly more intense purr came forth, as if in answer. As if to say "Yes, I'll come along to the fortress."

Sage was not wholly surprised then, when before dawn the following morning, the Lynx appeared as she descended the treehouse ladder. She had put him out the night before, reminding him, "Be here in the morning, Lynx. I'll wait for you."

She was not surprised, but very pleased at the sight of him. She never took the awesome animal's presence for granted. They walked together, almost silently. One of Sage's favorite things about the forest was the air. She loved the way it smelled. She loved the sweet green smell of the pine and fir trees. It was that crisp, alive smell, and just breathing it infused her with inspiration and health. How comforting it was to be walking along, in near darkness, with a large wildcat at her side. Sage's eyesight wasn't just keen in daylight; it was also keen in the dark. As a child, she used to proudly say, "I'm a cat. I can see in the dark."

Rough deer paths wove around everywhere in the forest. These paths were like roads to Sage. She knew them well, and found them easy to travel upon. Her strong leather boots, last year's birthday gift, still had thick soles. Her birthday was November first, the middle day of Samhain, the sacred Druid festival. The Druids (Druid meant magician in Gaelic) believed that the last day of October (All Hallows Eve) and the first two days of November were when the veil between the worlds was at its most thin. To a Druid, Sage was born at the absolutely most auspicious time of the year. So she was very proud of her birthday, though her parents knew nothing of this lore. She had found it out in her own wily way.

The sun started rising. They were getting closer to the fortress. Ravens squawked in nearby trees. And finally, the clearing. The stone fortress was situated in a fairly large clearing within the forest. It was beautiful in its slightly ruinous state, with overgrown flowers, ferns, and moss coating its base stones. It was a perfect square with a turreted tower at each corner. The great door was of wide wood panels, arched and pointed at the top, with decorative iron adorning the hinges. At almost twice her height, it was the grandest door Sage had ever seen.

Do I knock? Sage was thinking, but no need. Suddenly Artos was there. He had come silently around the corner from the front right tower. "My Lady," he said as he bowed.

Three

LESSONS IN THE COURTYARD

"Artos." She said in greeting, nodding her head.

"I see you have brought our silent forest friend." He gently patted the big cat. The Lynx moved close to Artos' leg, brushing his fur against him, as cats do when they like someone.

"Let us enter," Artos said. It was like being admitted into a dream. Sage followed Artos after he had heaved open the massive door about two feet. The three walked through a tunnel-like entrance hall, all stone. The hall was about ten strides long, and then they were out in the sunshine again—the courtyard. Sage loved it, even though it was utterly overgrown, with grasses long and unkempt. She took note immediately of the lichen covered marble benches in the center of the courtyard. Each was a semi-circle, and they faced each other.

"You see Sage I want you to understand about infinity." The voice which spoke came from Artos but seemed to originate from a different source, as if some spirit were speaking through him.

"I can not conceive of a more beautiful concept than infinity. It is so allowing. It has its own life. It gives you the gift of being able to spread out completely, utterly. You can take an idea, and if it is pure, know that the idea can become endless."

"I want you to know, Sage, that your spirit is infinite. There is not one boundary that is stopping you. There are no boundaries in all of infinity."

"Please sit," he gestured to the lichen clad bench. The pale green, mosslike growths seemed to be almost an upholstery, and Sage gladly sat on it, thankful for the strength of marble, and the life of lichen. Because she knew: *I am being taught.*

"Sage. God lives at the end of infinity. And there is no end. I know this is a paradox. But I know you can understand. God pulls us through all of infinity. But only very few are aware. You are. I just know."

"For those who are aware, it becomes their sanctuary. And it also becomes their duty, destiny, task, to take their awareness as far into infinity as it can go."

"This requires that you start listening to your inner core. Listening to your core starts out a very subtle thing, though ultimately it sounds like thunder."

A break ensued, during which Sage remembered to breathe in as much air as she could hold. Artos was seated on the other bench, facing her. The cool clean air filtered in through her nostrils. And the truth that he spoke, O Soothsayer, reverberated in her bones and soul.

She wasn't young anymore. Rather, the wisdom of ancientness awakened in her, and though she did not understand his speech mentally, she knew it was all her language.

Artos. She had thought he was just a man. A good man, a kind one, but mortal. She had expected none of this, yet it was the finest thing she had ever heard. There was a music behind those words, that danced through them.

"Ah, my beautiful owl." An owl had entered the picture, landing upon the wide, seatlike edge of the battlements. It observed them, seated down below. "Not really my owl, but my friend," said Artos. Sage observed Artos' face. His skin was perfectly smooth, seemingly poreless and rather silvery. His eyes were blue, warm, but that icy color. He had a kind face. She spoke: "Artos, from what

I have read, you remind me of the magician Merlin."

"This is a deep compliment, and I must admit, proudly, that I have Merlin's blood in me."

Merlin's blood! That meant he was a descendant. "You are then his descendant?" she inquired.

"Remember, about my relative, Selchie. They were at Avalon together. Merlin is also a distant relative of mine. Therefore I can say I have his blood in me."

Artos changed the subject. "Before we speak of the cards," he glanced to see if she had brought them, as she had hidden them under her tunic, "tell me what you think of this place." By this time he had regained his usual voice.

Sage revealed the colorful pouch, with its red, orange, pink and blue yarn diamonds, placing it next to her on the bench. She looked around more. They were surrounded by stone. How safe she felt here. She looked more closely. Two blue glittering dragonflies flew together nearby. The owl was watching her. Sage stood and walked to an interior wall, and observed the mossy stones that met the ground. *"Where there is moss, I am welcome,"* she thought. The stones were so thick in moss that some had grass and ferns growing out of them.

"Well, Artos. There is sun here. And grass and moss and lichen. And stone, and our animal friends. We are open to the sky. This courtyard is like a room that is alive, with no ceiling. For me, it is heaven."

"And can you hear the waves? If you listen very closely, you can just make them out."

She listened and heard it. The thunder-like rumbling of the sea.

"Now, Lady, have you chosen any cards?"

"A beaver. A beaver in a lake, and it was swimming. Lots of trees." She spoke, seeing it in her mind.

"Do you remember anything about the water, Sage?"

She tilted her head sideways, her face upturned slightly, and closed her eyes. Inside of her mind she imagined the card there. "It is rather golden on the surface. It looks warm."

"The beaver is important but the most important thing is the water. Water depicts change, movement. Water is an amazing thing, it is a paradox because it is a flexible solid. And what about the beaver?"

"He—or—she seemed happy. Diving in and out of the water and swimming around."

"Beavers are very kind and patient animals. They build loving families and strong homes. You see, Sage, these cards are mirrors for the beholder. Most of us have been taught to believe in limited meanings. You must expand your view of meanings, and that is partly what these cards are about. The cards are to assist you in discovering your destiny. For the discovery of one's destiny is such a miraculous thing. Not all will want to discover it, for it can be daunting. But there is nothing more inspiring than to know your true, God given purpose in life."

Chills were running along Sage's back because she understood, and could feel her own destiny looking right at her.

"First, let us go through the cards—have you looked at them all yet?"

"I have not—I—was so amazed by the one I did pick."

"Right," said Artos. "May I have the deck?" She handed it to him, and one by one he began to pass them back to her, slowly, picture side up. Within each card there was movement, some fast, some slow. Trees swayed. Eyes blinked. Wind blew, and water moved.

"We have Thunder and Lightning (little lightning bolts cracked through the sky, and the sound of thunder issued from the card); a cave; a wisewoman; a wiseman; the sea; the sun; jewels of gold and precious gems; rain; a bed; one in meditation; fire; air; instinct and intuition; a winding path; a bird in flight; stairs; stars; the moon; Stonehenge; a horse; a dog; a wild cat; magic; faith and truth; a castle; a great sailing ship; rocks with moss and lichen; music; silence; love; a lake with trees; a mountain; destiny and infinity. It's meant to be that there are thirty-three."

Artos observed Sage's young face, and addressed something that he knew was in her mind: "Do not be overwhelmed by the number of cards. The number has nothing to do with your art of reading them. Your extra-sensory perception will be your greatest guide; that is why I encouraged you to listen to your inner core."

"How did you know I had extrasensory perception, Artos?"

"Since I have it myself, I see it in you, that is all."

It sounded sensible enough, and she believed him. Still, it seemed like Artos knew an awful lot about her. But she trusted him, so it was no matter.

"You have now seen each card, and though they are changing all the time, the essence remains constant. It seems very lucky that you saw that beaver in the lake and tree card; you may never see it again. Now, there are some groupings. There are three cards of direction: the stairs, the path, and destiny and infinity. The stairs—when one pulls that card, it suggests that the person either needs to go deeper into a matter, which would be to go down, or that he is heading towards inspiration, which would be an ascent."

Sage let him keep talking because she knew it was just too early to ask questions. She raised her eyebrows at him and nodded, as if to urge him on.

"To draw the path card—it implies being well on the way to knowing the direction of one's destiny. And the destiny and infinity card—how very auspicious. For this means that the person already knows his destiny, either consciously or unconsciously. Now, knowing your destiny does not necessarily mean that you are living it or being it or practicing it. Many people semi-consciously sense their destinies, but are too afraid and so do not pursue them. This always leads to some level of discontent. It is those who observe their discontent, and realize it has something to teach them and do not try to ignore it, who will ultimately be aligned with their specific destiny or path in life and thus will be fulfilled."

"The homing, or nurturing cards of introspection are the castle, the cave and the bed. The castle is the place of maturity, elegance, success, and manifestation. The cave focuses on solitariness, silence, and wildness. The bed is the womb, for safety and healing. There are three primary animals: the cat, dog and horse. You must never underestimate the power of animals and the examples set by them. The dog represents loyalty, protection, and forgiveness, and giving people or situations another chance. The cat represents freedom and detachment, because it does not become overly attached to anyone or anyplace. It also represents the endless power of wildness." They both took a moment to look at the Lynx, who was curled up and sunning himself at Sage's feet. He was a beautiful cat, with his thick coat, tufted ears and huge paws.

Artos continued. "The horse symbolizes one's ability to move, travel and journey with strength. Can you hear more now, Lady?" But even as he said it, Artos noted that her face was rapt, and even the cat seemed to be paying attention. A few small clouds had entered overhead, but the day was growing nicely warm. A perfect day, and place, for teaching, Artos thought. And I haven't even showed her inside the fortress yet!

"My lord, there is nothing I would rather hear now, but more of this."

"Very well. Lake, sea, and rain are water cards. You have chosen the lake yourself. These three suggest solidity combined with flexibility, or an inherent strength that is open to change. The lake is more safe but less risky than the sea. The lake represents curiosity. The sea is less safe but more risky than the lake. It represents chance and the desire to discover. Risk is good, we get results from it. Rain is for cleansing, moisturizing, nourishing. And trees, which are on the lake card, represent flexibility and grounding, rootedness. They can also signify shelter."

"Faith and truth, instinct and intuition, and love are the invisibles. The paradox here is, while they may seem invisible or intangible, they are all powerful creative forces that ultimately have very visible and tangible effects. To have faith you must have trust. To trust is to be aligned with the truth, the vibration that emanates from your core. You can spend your whole life heightening your awareness of that vibration. Instinct and intuition represent choices and action, combining the two most powerful forces that make decisions—your heart and your higher mind. And love—when love takes over, no amount of resistance from your mind will matter. That is the power that love, especially true love, has. At times the mind thinks it has to fight rather than to surrender. But your heart, and love, will win you over. And once you surrender, then you can truly enjoy the gift that love eternally gives."

They were ensconced in the warm morning air. Sage still looked enraptured, so Artos continued.

"Stonehenge, the mountain, and rocks connote solidity and security. Stonehenge is the circle of megaliths, representing infinity and power. A mountain would be something we strive for, almost a goal or an intention. It is also symbolic of paradox because: if you are looking at the mountain you view its beauty, yet once you climb the mountain to know it, the view changes to that of where you were at the outset of the climb. And rocks symbolize acceptance. They readily accept snow, rain, sun and all variations of the above without changing. Moss and lichen," he glanced up to see her face, "are equated with security and comfort."

"Sun, stars and the moon are the celestials. The sun literally equals heat and light, and it also suggests insight and awareness. The moon is our night light; it represents support, or light, given in times of darkness, and assurance that if your intention is strong, you will be shown the way. The stars and planets are our reminder of the 'Great Picture'—we know there is so much more out there. These bright sparks can pull us out of becoming too self absorbed."

"Meditation is a reminder to breathe. Meditation can lift you away from worries and distractions. You can even experience a floating feeling of being disconnected from your body. Daily practice gives one daily truth, a consistent reminder to be aware of the greater picture, of God, of love. Jewels of gold and precious gems represent giving and receiving. Fire spurs action and represents one's inner power felt in the gut area. Air is for health, and breathing air is a guide for hearing your inner self or core."

As Artos spoke, Sage looked at the corresponding cards. The magic card had a female magician casting a spell out of doors, with the moon a sliver in the twilight sky. "Magic represents having the mind of a child. Magic represents a complete lack of rules or boundaries in the mind, rather, genuine awareness that anything Is possible. A wiseman and a wisewoman are within all of us, because we all have male and female facets. But to draw one of those cards means that that part of you is emerging—though it might mean that a wiseperson is sending you a message."

"The bird in flight is about levitation, flying, and astral projection. Silence is many things, and there are many types. Silence represents quietness and solitude and peace; it can also be your mirror. Above all though, silence is beauty. The great sailing ship is about floating and thus about the importance of balance. Music can mirror the most inspired parts of one's soul. Music can remind you of who you really are at your most powerful level, especially music that reflects aspects of yourself which make you feel high and alive, or relaxed and soothed."

"Finally, thunder and lightning. This is divine inspiration: God is speaking to you." There was a pause.

"I know what you mean, Artos. All my life whenever I have heard thunder, I have had vibrations of power all through my body. Thunder has always been my highest, most revered sound."

Artos looked at her closely. *Very good,* he thought. *This is just what I needed to hear from the girl. Now I know for certain that she is indeed the right one for the cards.* Her alignment with thunder and lightning was the sign he had been waiting for.

"About your inner core—most people do not think in terms of having one. But we each do. When you can walk from that core, talk from that core, Be from that core, then, my Lady, you are impenetrable. Your space, the field of energy all around your physical body, will be like a wall of protection. And in knowing this vast and deep safeness, you will be able to blossom into All that You Are. I can not urge you enough to become aware of your inner core, and to ever heighten your awareness of it. This is where truth is, this is where God is, this is where peace is."

He looked at her intently. "There is a grandeur that lives in all of us, Sage. A Majesty. For we, humans, are so creative. There is such a wealth of newness to be manifested. There are such limitless combinations of all that already is."

Four

WITHIN THE CARD'S WORLD

The cards, piled loosely, stared up at Sage and Artos. Each reality was separate, contained within the card which housed it. It was real in there, she was absolutely convinced of it. It seemed that she could enter the scene if she so desired. But she did not know the magic word, if there was one, and then she heard it: "Parasamgate." It came from Artos.

"It is a Sanskrit word—that is the sacred language of the ancient, learned Hindus. It means 'gone beyond the beyond.' And you must utter it, Sage, to enter the realm of the card."

"But first you tap in to the magic vein."

She looked at him, already knowing essentially what he meant. "You mean, sink

34

down into that wavelength that is the inception of creativity—where lives the very matrix of magic."

Artos stared at her. "Right." It takes much unveiling of the mind to access that wavelength, and somehow, she had already done it. *It is because she is wise,* he thought.

Sage was sitting on her bench, upon the lichen-clad marble, holding within her hand the card which contained rocks covered with moss and lichen. The tree in the foreground of the card had those growths on it as well. A stream trickled along. There were trees everywhere, lining the edge of the stream. "I want to go in here," she said to Artos.

"Anyone can say 'Parasamgate.' But tapping into the magic vein is another matter entirely. It takes much discipline and mind practice to let go of the fears which keep one from living within that deep place."

"Try it, then, Lady. I bid you good luck, and will guard you and await your return."

Sage glanced around her. There were the stone walls of the fortress, the clear blue sky, sweet fresh air, Artos' blue eyes and silver hair. Strangely, she thought she heard a dog barking. She held the card and stared into it, watching the stream water flow, and tree boughs and leaves swaying in the wind. She breathed deeply, accessing the magic vein. It felt like an expansion of spirit, like wisdom and joy and great beauty. Once she felt truly ready, she uttered "Parasamgate."

Sage's human body remained in the fortress courtyard with Artos. He gently pulled her off the bench and laid her down on the grass, as the Lynx promptly came and sat right next to her head, as if to imply: *I am the guardian.*

Artos now held the card which had been in Sage's hand. Within it he saw a blue and purple dragonfly flitting about, then landing upon a big mossy rock. The dragonfly dissolved. In its place was a pale ghost of Sage. *Ah, yes, the dragonfly is a transformer,* Artos remembered.

Sage held up her hand to the light of the sun and she could see through it. She looked down. She could see right through her body. But she was not in the least scared. Her body was just a thin film. But she had total awareness of her situation. She knew she was within the world of the card.

Everything was talking to her. The moss, the trees, the water of the stream, the lichen, and the leaves emitted together a melodic harmony. So she focused on one thing, the moss upon which she sat. She focused her hearing, to discern the moss's own voice from that of the rest. It was humming. The sound was soft, and muted and furry, but the more she listened, the more she could make it out. *Perhaps if I ask it a question, it will answer me directly.*

"O Holy Moss," Sage said out loud, "what are the secrets of the future of Avalon?"

At first she heard a muffled, furry, whirring sound directed at her and—perhaps because the rules of reality were different here—she slowly began to decipher the meaning of the moss's language. "In the beginning of Time there were always magic worlds. When people came, the first people, they lived in the magic worlds and knew it was normal. Avalon was the last magic world to be displaced from what you think is reality. Avalon is still linked to your reality by a thread, and you will find that thread."

"We mosses and lichens are of the oldest life forms still surviving on this planet. So I am from the beginning of the world. I am a part of your consciousness from the beginning of the Earth. You and I are the same, Sage."

The oldness of the moss, like roots, was a foundation of comfort for her mind. Its very ancientness felt like home. When something has been around that long, it knows everything; it is wise; it has witnessed all of the rises and falls.

"Behold the unique beauty of this world, Sage. You think you are inside of a card, but alas: You could stay right here forever, for this is as true and real a world as that one you just left."

Glancing around her, Sage saw and felt that this world seemed actually *more* real and true than the one she had just left. Perhaps it was her lack of fear. Since here, she had not one atom of fear in her consciousness, and her ability to interpret beauty and wisdom was greatly expanded. Beauty was a liquid thing here, dripping from the boughs of trees, twinkling off leaves, being exuded from the very water of the stream. Visible vibrations flowed forth from the mosses, and the air itself held magical molecules of oxygen, which popped open upon her breathing them in, so with each inhalation she felt ignited with the highest level of life.

A blue and purple dragonfly flitted along, landing just next to her. He was so light, the moss could barely feel him.

───────

From Artos' point of view, Sage was still a shadow, a ghost sitting on a mossy rock, staring around her. He had been watching the whole time, staring into the card as he sat upon his marble bench in the fortress courtyard. When he saw the dragonfly alight upon the rock next to her, he knew it would not be long before her spirit came back into her human body.

Indeed, her ghost faded from view within the card; the dragonfly flew off, and what looked to be the *same* dragonfly suddenly came to land upon Sage's brow, as she lay on the courtyard grasses.

Her long lashes blinked at the brightness of the sun, and the Lynx nudged her face with his muzzle, tickling her skin with his whiskers. She slowly reached an arm up to pet his fur. In her super openminded awareness, Sage realized this: It was the absence of fear that allowed her to see the true depths of beauty and life within things.

Then she remembered the moss's furry, whirring voice: *"Avalon is still linked to your reality by a thread, and you will find that thread."*

Whatever happens in the mind when one's consciousness shifts (as in, from sleep to wakefulness) happened now, within Sage, and she adjusted back to the life of the courtyard. She was so perfectly full and contented with her experience that she did not want to reduce it to words, and luckily Artos suspected that. It is often the case when one has magical experiences.

Five

INSIDE THE FORTRESS

Suddenly Sage jumped up. Mesmerized as she had been by the uplifting teachings of Artos, and by the exotic otherworld within the card, now she wanted to stretch her legs and take deep breaths of the warm fresh air.

"Now then, Lady, you have seen and heard much. How about investigating the interior of this dwelling?"

"Please, Artos. Allow me to walk around in this courtyard for a few moments. Then may we go inside."

He smiled upon her rosy, happy face. "Right. And I will bring you some food."

As Artos went inside, Sage began to walk around, with the Lynx following her. Actually he walked with her, as a human would do, though at times he would stop and sniff. Sage was thrilled and exhilarated. She loved the cards. She loved the teachings. She trusted Artos. It seemed like her life was opening up, and that the sun was truly shining on her, bestowing her with goodness. It was so quiet, and she could hear the distant waves of the sea churning against the shore. Also she could hear different birds chirping and squawking. Her favorite was the cooing of the dove. The coos always came in threes. *Birds always sound excited in the spring*, she thought. She stopped and stretched her legs and her arms, taking in deep breaths of the air. *Even the air feels alive*, she thought. *It is feeding me.*

Artos returned with two red apples in one hand and a small block of cheese in the other. He handed one apple and the cheese to Sage. "From my town," he said. The cheese was hickory smoked, Sage noticed upon smelling it. That smoky smell always had a positive effect on her. It reminded her of warmth and fires.

"Let us in, Lady." He gestured back toward the tunnel-like entrance hall where they had first entered the courtyard. Halfway through the hall on the left, there was a beautiful oak door with much intricate carving. In the very center of the door was carved a dragon. Artos opened it with ease and Sage could tell it was used often. They entered a room.

The ceiling was low, with wooden beams supporting it. The windows had diamond shaped panes. From the moment Sage crossed over the threshold, she could feel the room even more than she could see it. It was as if the room itself had a spirit—not a human spirit—but one that lived within the very wood of the walls. This spirit exuded peace, and the peace was visible even in the room's objects: the blue and white dishes in the cupboard; an oriental carpet upon the flagstone floor; the candlesticks laden with wax drippings upon a long carved wooden table.

Here silence was a sound. Birds were chirping outside, and their chirps mingled with the harmony within. What was it? Was it the china bowl full of potatoes upon the ancient sideboard? Was it the wreath of dried berries, and the spiral seashells resting upon the mantle above the brick fireplace—or the mirror reflecting all of it back at her?

The room, though in a fortress, had the feel of a cottage. There was floral fabric upon the sofa and settee in one corner, and a green painted bookcase laden with leather volumes. Through one window Sage could see the white blossoms of a pear tree. Tiny oil paintings of nature scenes dotted the walls. A blue glass vase of magenta sweet pea blossoms sat in the sunlight upon the wooden table, and chairs that looked to befit a king and queen sat at the carved table's head and foot.

Sage wanted to pinpoint where the meditative, soothing feelings were coming from, and finally she decided it could only be love. Whoever decorated this space must have been full of love while she was doing it.

"Artos." She murmured. "I adore it."

"I knew you would, Sage. It is a place befitting a lady like yourself."

If Sage had not felt almost a fatherlike caring from Artos, she may have blushed. But she knew, *"Artos just understands me."*

"There are many rooms in this fine home. Let us walk through them, so you can see."

He led her through room after room, all with little diamond windows, all with the same touches of elegance and love she had witnessed in the first room. Bedrooms, sitting rooms; a library. Occasionally she would glance through the windows facing the courtyard. She liked seeing the marble benches in the courtyard, and knowing, "I have just been there, and now I am here, looking out." She could almost see the ghosts of herself and Artos, with the cards out there in the sun.

"Who keeps this castle, lord?"

"A very wealthy man who is indebted to me. My payment, or reward, is to use this property as I wish, for as long as I wish, without intrusion. As if it were truly mine, except I do not have to pay for it." He smiled, a bit ruefully. "I did pay for it, in a way other than money."

"So you live here?"

"Actually, lady, I live in a cave, but do spend some time here. Since I do not live here, and it is an available residence, I thought I would offer to you the opportunity—of taking a room here."

A bit of silence ensued, as Sage was stunned by glory. Her face lit up; then, without making a show of her amazement, Sage accepted this new good luck. "Artos, I am honored, and I will think about it for a day. But I am sure I will accept."

He nodded. And as he paused to look out the next window at something, Sage's mind was already at work, picking out her bedroom. There had been one, with a pale rose colored coverlet on the little bed. The diamond window in this tiny room was almost right above the head of the bed. *The fresh air would waft in at night for me to smell,* she thought. There had been a small bookcase, filled with leather volumes; an ornate oriental carpet on the floor; a tiny desk and chair; another larger chair in the corner, covered also in a dusty rose colored cover. *Rose and stone go well together.* As she was remembering the room, Artos' voice checked her back to the moment. "Have you decided?" He smiled, and she could tell he was reading her mind.

"May we go back to see the rose room, the tiny one?"

"The tiny room—the child's room." He looked at her. "Right. You like caves too, do you not, lady?"

She smiled and nodded. Indeed, the rose room was like a cave for a child. They retraced their steps. Closer and closer they came to the room. Finally, they reached the door, which was ajar. Sage entered first, and was about to state her pleasure that there was a fireplace, when she noticed something that hadn't been there before—a black cat. The cat moved from a curled up sleeping position to a dignified sitting position, right before Sage's amazed eyes. This wasn't an ordinary cat. It had deep yellow eyes. The cat looked at her as though it already knew her. Something about the cat's eyes made Sage feel peaceful, and safe.

"This cat is from Tintagel," came Artos' voice, though Sage's eyes were still fixed on the cat's. "He followed me to these woods years ago. I see he has taken residence in this fortress—though before today, lady, I have not seen him here."

The cat was on the bed, at the foot. Sage went to pet him. He had thick, short fur. "This is just the kind of cat I've always wanted."

Artos was smiling benevolently at the two. "I take it this is your new room?"

"I suppose I don't need the day to decide. Yes, Artos, I would love for this to be my room." Quite suddenly Sage realized that she was very tired. Though it was still early, it felt like a full day had passed.

"Would it be all right for me to have a nap at this time, sir?"

As Artos drifted away, out the door, Sage was overcome with gladness about being able to nestle into her new room right away. She walked over to her bed, with the black cat on it. Again she petted him. She already knew it was her cat. "You're actually a charcoal cat," she said very softly to him. He did have quite dark gray fur. Sage sat on her desk chair to remove her boots. Then she folded back the covers and got into the bed. *This is grand,* she thought. *I even have a cat to keep my feet warm.* She snuggled up tightly in the small bed, briefly wondering if this was all real.

And after a while she dreamed. She dreamed of a hat that she had and when she put it on, she got a sharp pain right at her hairline. Removing the hat, looking inside she saw a spider, and realized it had bitten her. She looked in the mirror. There was a small hole in her head.

Sage kept sleeping for a while after the dream. When she woke up hours later, she was full of peace. She thought: *There is nothing for all the world like peace.* Then a voice spoke inside of her mind and it said: "Peace lives in you." She thought of Artos saying that she must start listening to her inner core. *I think that was my core, talking to me.*

The bed was so warm. The cat was still there. Afternoon sunlight streamed through the window. She stared at the bookshelves. She could just make out a title: *Animal*

Teachings: Interpretations. The book was dark green and leather bound.

Then came a soft knock on the door. "Artos?"

"Sage." He entered the room only slightly. "I believe it is time for your next lessons. Let us meet in the kitchen." He smiled warmly upon her.

"What is this book about?" She had climbed out of bed and was holding up the animal book.

"Ah, my lady, you are so clever. Please bring the book with you to the kitchen. It is something you will need to read and study, if you are to be deft with the Cards."

With that he was gone. Sage felt refreshed and full of inspiration. Now that she knew Artos, trust was entering back into her heart and growing. She had lost much trust at the hands of her father. Being treated with cruelty over and over again, day after day, had worn down her trust. Now, feeling the peace that trust brings made her happy in a way she had never known. And again, it felt like her inner core was talking to her, but it was more of a feeling than a voice. The feeling was: *You can trust this happiness. It is pure.*

Sage found herself with her boots back on, book in hand, and in the kitchen in mere minutes, so eager she was to continue learning from her new teacher.

He was sitting at the table, the big oak one, with a very contemplative look on his silvery face. Even though it was daytime, he had lit the candles, so there were five bright flames in the otherwise dimly lit kitchen. Sage sat down across from Artos. He looked at her in a mysterious way, which prompted her to state and question: "Artos, who *are* you?"

Way in the back of Artos' pupil, there was a twinkle. Sage knew that she couldn't ask about it. But the part of her that could hear God understood that twinkle, and seeing it resonated with her, and she got chills down her back and arms, though the day was still warm.

Artos did not answer her question. Instead, he began. "Magic is the spontaneous manifestation of your immediate desire. Doubt is the residue of negative psychic archetypes. So, Sage, have you learned anything from listening to your core?"

She was still thinking about what he said about magic. Now she considered the question. "The more I tell myself to listen, the more I feel rather a warm, trusting vibration deep in my heart. This vibration sways me in the right direction. Already, the vibration reminds me not to worry, not to fear."

"So true! You will do well to give up worry and fear. To worry is to strangle; it strangles the mind and instincts. And fear—it is a waste. We misuse fear—God gave it to us for protection's sake. Unfortunately, fear has taken on too much power. That is what I meant by 'Doubt is the residue of negative psychic archetypes.' Doubt is fear; archetypes are beliefs or memories that live in the collective human mind for generation upon generation. Realize the negative archetypes that live in you; that is the first step in releasing them or transmuting them."

"What would be an example of a negative archetype?"

"One is that everything must be done quickly. This pushes people to excessive speed, and they miss the messages of their instincts, and of God, along the way. Those messages make life, and tasks, more creative and enjoyable."

Sage sat deep in thought. She smelled the smell of old oak in that room, and if stone had a scent, she could smell that too. And a faint crisp apple aroma. There was a lot to learn. But Artos seemed patient.

"Artos, I had a dream about a spider, that bit me." She told him all of it, and where the bite occurred.

"Spiders are weavers. They symbolize the ways that we weave our daily lives and our destinies. And the top part of your head is your crown. This is the energy center where divine light source energy enters your body, infusing you with God. So, I would say a dream about a weaver biting your crown and leaving a hole is an auspicious thing."

She tilted her body so she could look out the window. There were many trees nearby. "I need air, my lord." She stood to go out of doors.

"Why don't you have a look around this place, Sage."

She went out, through the door with the carved dragon, then through the door with the decorative iron, and noted how different the air smelled from hours earlier. There are few things as magical as the smell of spring air. Earlier it was sweet and warm. Now it was peaceful and balmy. The Lynx was nowhere to be seen, but that was normal. She knew he could turn up again at any time. It was still clear, and sunny, but growing cooler as sunset drew near. *I suppose I am sleeping here tonight,* Sage thought. Suddenly she wondered about Artos—*would he sleep here as well?* Especially on her first night, she did not want to sleep alone in the large fortress. *What if there were ghosts?*

Many of the trees were carpeted with lichen. In some areas of the tree trunks, ferns grew out of the moss which coated the bark. It was a lovely sight. *Why do I love moss so much?* she pondered. Just the sight of it made her want to be near it, to press on it gently and feel its furry resistance. *Earth fur,* she called it in her mind. Plus, the color was quite appealing, for it was such an emerald green. A red squirrel bolted out of a hole in the tree closest to her. It chittered and ran back inside. *With little animals, a tree hole or a hollow log is a home,* she marveled. She thought about how satisfied animals were with the basics that had been given to them.

Now it was night. Artos was staying in the fortress too, a few rooms away. How quiet the fortress was. Sage seemed to be feeling the people who had lived there before. She wondered about the girl who had lived in her new room. *The books*, she thought. *I can tell by the books.* She stared at the volumes, while sitting on a small stool. One book on Stonehenge caught her attention especially. Withdrawing it, she flipped it open, and it revealed drawings of the awesome rocks. Megaliths, it said. Giant upright stones made of limestone. Still a mystery how they got there. She thought: *There is nothing wrong with mystery. I like it that no one can figure out how the stones got there. Maybe it was an act of magic.*

With the stone temple of Stonehenge in her mind, Sage snuggled into the bed, with the charcoal cat warming her feet. She was thinking briefly that it was a good thing spring was here. The fortress was a bit chilly. But the bed and the cat were warm enough, and she slept soundly. Some stress even escaped her body during the night, so upon waking, Sage felt different than usual. She felt rather calmer inside, and looking forward to the day. She had learned to fear the day, from living at home—because as long as it was day, her father was awake, and as long as he was awake, he was most always torturous. It felt good to not have to fear the day anymore.

She leaped out of bed and threw open the window with diamond shaped panes. *Oh, the air, it smells so sweet! Perhaps from an early flowering tree.* She couldn't wait to be outside, and dressed quickly, letting herself out of the nearest exterior door—which lead right into the courtyard. It was glorious spring, and Artos was seated on one of the marble benches.

"Sage! Good morning. How would you like to go to Stonehenge today? It's something you should really see."

At first it felt shocking that Artos was rather reading her mind. But then, it actually felt like the most normal thing in the world.

"You must be able to see inside of my mind, my lord, for I went to sleep envisioning Stonehenge."

"Perfectly timed then! And fine weather for riding. I have a horse for you."

Sage was glowing. All of her life this was something she had wanted to see. All she knew was that it was colossal and sacred. Even if she had wanted to, Sage probably could not have explained why Stonehenge meant so much to her. Knowing Artos, there was some special treat involved. And a horse...she had ridden sparsely as a child, but she loved horses. She began to grow accustomed to the good luck that had befallen her. But never would she get used to her gratitude. She felt grateful every hour of the day. Every day felt like a relief, to be out of her father's house and out into the free world.

And so they set out across the wild moors.

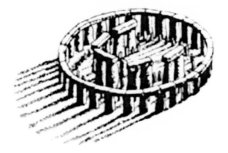

Six

STONEHENGE

Sage was not really prepared for the Lynx following them. She would think she caught glimpses of a lynx, here and there, behind a tree. Finally, she knew; and then, by the end of the first day, around a small fire Artos had constructed, the animal made his full presence known. Some cats are like that, rather like dogs, and they will follow their loved ones.

She was warmed inwardly by the animal's presence. She was touched deeply that he had followed them. How she loved this cat. Surrounded by heath brush, they sat by the fire, the three of them, and Sage stroked the Lynx's thick coat. He purred, and it was loud. She found it such a reassuring sound. *Why does cat purring comfort me so?* Sage asked herself. *Maybe the cat is happy, and that makes me happy.*

Artos spoke. "One of the most important things in life you can do is show intent. This builds up, and can manifest in the future. For example, you may intend in earnest to be happy and calm. In the moment of your active intention, perhaps you won't feel those feelings. But at some later time, happiness and calmness will befall you, unexpectedly. So patience is required."

Her chiseled cheeks glistened at their highest points with the light moisture of the spring air. "Yes, this makes sense. I have always dreamed of a life of magic, and those dreams were my intent. Now I see that with you, my cards, and the Lynx, I have found the beginnings of magic."

The fire crackled. The Lynx stretched. *No doubt, he is thinking of his nighttime antics,* Sage thought.

"You see those stars out there, Sage? They are tiny suns. Crack your mind and brain open beyond thoughts. The totality of time is enclosed in one single moment. Hence all past and future events are happening simultaneously."

"Always choose action and movements of the highest order. The more you align with your inner core signals, the wiser will be your choices."

She regarded him, his face, his wisdom. "When you say these things, I feel like I've always known them, but forgotten them until you reminded me." She was then still for long moments. "It is so quiet here, Artos. Silence is one of my favorite sounds."

"Part of this beautiful silence is the hiss and crack of the fire, and the purring of the Lynx."

"Artos, I love to be away, away from the town, away from the people. Otherwise I would not be hearing this sacred nothingness."

She is old before her time, Artos thought. "Yes, this is why I cave dwell."

"And I treehouse dwell." She giggled.

"Though now, lady, it seems you may fortress dwell."

"If it is meant to be. I have an instinct though, that our trip to Stonehenge may take longer than we thought."

She began her sleep with her body between warm skins and her head on the Lynx. Eight hours later the light of the morning sun began landing on every single thing it could touch, thus making things visible. She opened her eyes. Mistiness covered the land, and as the sunlight reflected off each and every particle of mist, the air itself glowed. And then the unthinkable happened. The Lynx was

56

meowing, and rather growling. At first it sounded normal to her; then it changed. The guttural meows gradually turned into words in her mind. She could understand the Lynx.

He said: "My friend, you are a magician. Invent your own magic. That is your destiny." And then:

"Like lightning I will stand by you. That is my solemn offering."

Quite a long silence ensued, as Sage absorbed the miraculous.

Finally, Artos spoke: "So he's speaking to you, is he? I know the tone. I know not, however, what he said. Can you say?"

Sage slowly pulled herself into the moment at hand, looked at Artos' face, his eyes, and waited till he was in focus. "He told me I am a magician. For me to invent my own magic. That is my destiny. And he said 'Like lightning I will stand by you. That is my solemn offering.'" For the rest of her long life, Sage would never forget those words, in perfect order.

They all three sat together round the dying, unstoked fire, and the red embers seemed well aware of what was going on.

Then there was a touch of thunder, and a low rumbling in the western sky. "Taranis is speaking to you, lady." Her blank look prompted him. "The God of thunder and lightning. I dare say, that's your God."

The dawning of magicianhood, like oxygen, flowed in Sage's blood. The lessons of her life, most of them lies, slowly began leaking out of her young psyche.

She stood up. It felt like she was much taller than usual. Her head felt like it was two feet higher up in the air, and her brain felt connected by invisible strands to the infinite sky.

Artos stood up. She gazed at him, tilting her head slightly, and then looked him dead in the eyes, in the pupils. "Artos, you are Merlin reincarnated."

It was a simple sentence, but its truth was as deep and endless as heaven itself. In a part of himself that he barely knew existed, an awakening occurred. Within the awakening, Artos knew she spoke the truth.

"My Lord, lightning runs in my blood." The moment was alchemical. Sage would never be the same. She reached down and grabbed the card pouch. Still standing, she gently shuffled the cards. Finally, when she was ready, she drew one: the dog. He looked out at her and made sniffing motions. She held the card out for Artos to see.

"The dog represents loyalty and protection. It is quite evident to me why you have pulled this card. You were loyal to yourself. You left home in order to protect yourself."

Sage's face glowed. Artos already knew what she was feeling: the glee of the uncanniness that card choices could inspire. Novices with divination cards never cease to be amazed at how accurately the cards know.

"Look at him, Sage. Listen to him."

She seated herself upon a stone and held the card with both hands, intently looking into the dog's eyes. He looked up at her with such a tender gaze and she thought: *Only a dog could look at me like this.* Then in a soft bark that only Sage could hear, the dog within the card spoke to her.

"I have come to you over and over in life, even when you did not want to hear. I have come to you in the form of barking. I am your eternal reminder of loyalty. Your loyalty has stretched across time. You made a home for your loyalty within your heart, hence it has lived within you. As almost all others have given up on magic, you have remained loyal to it. You have protected it within you for centuries, and now magic is unveiled within you. Magic now rears its holy head. Only one who makes a home for magic will find it living within."

"So: with help from all light forces in and out of time; with help from all light forces upon earth and beyond it, you will bring Avalon back into the world as you know it. You are the vessel that was chosen."

When the truth settles upon a person, it has a calming effect. Some truths hold great responsibilities, and this was the case for Sage. But in the words of the dog there was such righteousness, doubt did not enter her mind, and she felt soothed. And she kept the dog's words to herself.

"Artos, we need to get on to Stonehenge. And we're quite close, aren't we?"

He nodded. Quietly they began to pack their gear. He thought what a blessing it was to be traveling in spring. Though the night was a bit cold, already the early morning sun was warming the air and land. And he liked the way Sage only spoke when necessary. It was good for her, to hold her energy so.

Once they began riding, the Lynx followed them. "You never wanted to name him?" Artos asked, gesturing to the cat.

"He is named. He was named from the beginning. Besides, I like the name Lynx."

Artos smiled to himself. It was a beautiful morning, and Stonehenge was only a few hours away. He knew something Sage did not know: that it was one thing to have seen drawings of Stonehenge, and it was quite another to see it live for the first time.

They rode on. Artos had provided for Sage a gentle white horse with kind eyes. The animal was a mass of warm muscle beneath her, and she loved being so high above the ground. The morning became brighter and warmer, and Artos had a surprise for Sage. It was the way they were to approach Stonehenge. One may arrive on flat land, seeing it in the distance, and it gradually becomes larger and larger as one nears it; thus there is time to adapt. Or, one can approach from behind a small hill, having not seen it at all yet, and as the top of the hill is reached—there the stones are suddenly, looking quite close, and quite astonishing. This was the way they were to approach.

Soon, he thought. Meantime the Lynx was following nearby but behind, in and out of trees. *Like lightning I will stand by you...* Sage heard in her mind. They began the ascent of the small hill. Closer and closer. She not expecting a thing, Artos aware of the build-up of tension inside of himself.

Suddenly Sage spoke: "What *is* that thing, it is so wild and strange! Those rocks are *huge*, I wonder...." Her voice trailed off as comprehension dawned. The skin of her arms and face prickled.

"Artos...it is awesome."

They descended, and came closer and closer, and all the while those stones became bigger and bigger. They dismounted. "I feel like these stones are my true home," she uttered. "I feel like I've been here before." By now they were standing inside of the primary circle of megaliths, heading into the inner horseshoe of trilithons. The stones comprising the trilithons were even taller than the stones of the primary circle. But instead of feeling daunted or humbled, Sage felt high and enlightened.

"This awesome pile of rocks is an astronomical device, a calendar. For thousands of years it has been used to track the movements of the sun, moon, and planets. It can track eclipses, equinoxes, and solstices. The main axis of Stonehenge points to the direction of sunrise on Midsummer Day." Artos pointed to the space between two of the outer megaliths.

"I want to stay within these rocks all day," she said, and sat down in the grass, staring around her. She saw a furry face behind one of the stones, peeking out. Sage thought: *What a funny cat. He knows no one else is here except us, yet still he is so elusive.*

"I feel like I know these rocks. Each one has its own wiseness." So much peace ran in her bones now. "These stones make me feel holy, Artos. Like all of the truth of the world is here. I could live here."

"Yes, it is a very magical monument. These stones were moved here from quite far away, by the process of levitation. That is why the books say their placement can't be explained. Few people anymore are willing to believe in magics like levitation."

"But you do?"

"Of course. It is simply one of the laws of magic, that gravity is not a constant. And once you know that, truly know it, you can walk on water."

Within the magic of those stones, walking on water actually did feel like something possible to her. "I feel so like I am home." She began walking all around amongst the stones, inspecting them, feeling them, even smelling them. Thin layers of living and dead lichen coated much of the stone. She weaved in and out of the sarsen circle of megaliths. The stones were almost four times her height.

"Someday, Artos, will you teach me all about this place?"

"There are few things I like to discuss more. So yes, certainly. But right now I just want you to feel it."

At the base of a stone that was being touched by sun, the cat slept. His body was curled up right against the rock. Sage marveled at his fur, how it blended in with the color of the stone.

"Artos, I am so happy."

Artos' silvery face reflected the morning sun. He looked at her with his kind blue eyes. "You know how, if you rapidly rub two pieces of dry wood together, you can create fire? The fire is in the wood. Similarly, magic is in everything. All physical matter is held together by magic. Because it lives in our brains. We think and imagine things, and thusly, particles come together to form our desires. Magic is the glue that holds molecules together."

"You see, Sage, all people are magicians. It's just that most are imagining, thus creating, things that they don't want. It was a very bad day when fear descended upon this planet. Fear is the killer of magic. Sadly, most people have believed the lies: To choose fearful thoughts over magical thoughts."

"Why did people start choosing fearful thoughts?"

"My child, to explain that I would have to begin my monologue on the church. Let us not ruin the morning with such a topic. Another time then—when your gut is stronger. You will have to learn this, for you to understand what befell Avalon."

She dropped the subject, knowing Artos would resume teaching it at the appropriate time. *It is good to be friends with a wiseman.*

"Your cat certainly likes that rock," he observed.

"Isn't he the finest, most precious, and most powerful thing? I feel like that cat contains everything good, all good things."

Then they ate food, some dried meats and fruits, and drank water from Artos' flask. Artos sat, leaning back against one of the giant stones.

"The smell of spring air alone is like a feeding, do you not think so, my lord?" Artos appreciated Sage's formality. *She is quite a queenly figure,* he thought.

"Yes, it is so sweet, Sage."

"I miss the sound of the sea. Remember when you said that all past, present, and future events are happening simultaneously? What did you mean?"

"It's very hard to explain within the context of a language, because language itself is limiting. But I can try. All events of all times are superimposed on top of each other, rather like layers. If you know how, you can feel and see people, animals and events of anytime or place. Please believe, it really is all happening simultaneously, if you view all of time as one totality."

"My mind must be stretched gradually, Artos." And then: "I'm going to choose a card." She sat on a fallen bluestone, as a chair, her head bent over and her knees pressed together. The old green velvet of her tunic was a rich backdrop for the red, orange, pink, and blue yarn diamonds of the card pouch. After shuffling, she chose. "It is the card of air." The card looked like the pale blue sky, with some small clouds moving slowly within it.

"Air is for health, and breathing air is a guide for hearing your inner self. Of all our natural gifts, air is the free-est. Remember when you said breathing spring air is like a feeding. That is actually a fact. You are feeding on fresh, newborn oxygen, which gives you the healthiest blood and therefore relaxes you. In a relaxed state, your core vibration is more accessible."

As Artos taught, Sage stared at the card. What a tiny little sky! But it looked so real. *It is real,* she reminded herself. Without meaning to, she mouthed "Parasamgate." And since she was already in the magic vein, the air card sucked her in. Suddenly she was aware of all its molecules. She had superlative vision, and could see that each air molecule was alive and multicolored in pastels, mostly pinks and greens. They looked like tiny shimmering bubbles. For the second time she realized that as she inhaled, it was these beautiful, plump molecules that delivered oxygen to her lungs. "Not all air is this fresh," said a voice. "Feel lucky that you live not in a city, where the molecules are not as pure and nutritive." The oxygen itself had personality; it was very giving. Sage could sense the generous spirit of it; it existed so that she and other animals could live.

Then she began hearing Artos' voice again:

"Did you just go *in* there?"

"Yes, my Lord, but only for mere moments..."

"Remember, you can live without food for weeks, without water for days, but you can only live without air for minutes."

She had never thought of it like that before. Somehow, Artos took the most basic things of life and presented them like the purest foods on the finest platters. Suddenly she felt very grateful again. "I suppose I've always taken air for granted."

"Most everyone does. But now you know. Fresh air is a human's most valuable resource. Let us hope it always remains free."

A wind had kicked up. Immediately Sage sought out a stone that protected her from its gusts. "It's almost like a house in here! Just without a roof." Saying this reminded her of the fortress courtyard. She felt a brief pang of missing that place which had just become her new home.

"I suppose we're off to Avalon soon, right Artos?" She looked at him for a reaction, and briefly saw such an intense sadness cross over his face; then it was gone.

"'Off to Avalon.' Well, lady, in this present moment I can't say I could take you to Avalon. But if you would, we could travel to Avalon back when it was alive and living. And what better portal through which to travel than this temple of Stonehenge."

Seven

MORGAN

"Now Sage, you must pay attention. All of your focus is required. You must make direct eye contact with me, and I will chant a spell. And when it works, we will be transported."

They were standing in the exact center of Stonehenge, within the sacred horseshoe of trilithons. Sage even thought she heard harps. Artos faced her straight on, with his hands on her shoulders, and the Lynx was between them at their feet.

"I speak to the blackness
of the pupil in your eye,
the blackness that
is
all of space
and all of eternity."

And then he was chanting things under his breath, she could not make them out, but it sounded ominous, cryptic, and otherworldly. He looked at her one last time. "Ready?" was all he said. She knew there was only one answer. "Yes," she nodded.

The power of the stones all around her, the warm sun beaming down, the Lynx's fur brushing her hand, these were her last awarenesses before she went blank in the mind, temporarily, until what seemed like hours later. She heard Artos' voice saying her name: "Sage. Lady, come to." And she could hear another voice, but the language was not of this earth.

"She's coming, I did not lose her." *Artos.* Then, the strange voice again, uttering the even more strange sounds. Sage loved the voice. It was weird, deep, holy.

"Ah...Merlin..." Sage was mumbling. Her eyes, just opening, slowly focused. "Artos!" And again the woman (faerie?) next to him uttered to him in the strange weird voice.

They were in Avalon when it was still alive. Sage blinked at the golden haze that was the entire sky. She stood on grass that was more green than in her usual world. She smelled the pink smell of apple blossoms. Sage stared at the faerie woman before her. She had brown hair and brown eyes and a blue crescent moon tattooed on her forehead. *She's the most beautiful thing I have ever seen,* thought Sage. *Already I love her.* The lady's face vibrated. For a second Sage saw a crown of holly leaves and berries on her head. Then it was gone. *She's a magic faerie woman,* Sage thought.

"Morgan," Artos said, and he gestured to the faerie woman.

"Morgan," Sage repeated.

Morgan reached out her small hands and took Sage's hands. She uttered her weird beautiful deep language at Sage. Sage did not know the words but could feel the meaning in her very core. It was a welcome of the highest degree, of the holiest degree, from this wisewoman.

"I've missed you all my life," Sage said. She did not intend to speak, but once it came out, she knew it was true. Artos translated for her. Morgan the faerie woman beamed. She nodded and again uttered the strange sounds. Sage hoped that Morgan would never speak English to her. She wanted to go on hearing that sound. It made her blood vibrate.

The two embraced. Morgan exuded a lavender smell. *She feels magical,* Sage thought. *Almost like she is not entirely solid, and could vanish at her will. And the way I understand the Lynx, I understand her. I can not speak her language; rather I understand it in a wordless way.*

Sage pulled back so that she could smile at Morgan. Morgan uttered as she looked directly at Sage. Artos said: "She's been waiting for you."

"I know," Sage said, nodding her head up and down. She had understood Morgan, even before Artos translated. But not the words. She just heard the vibrations and her mind somehow translated them.

The Lynx seemed instantly smitten with Morgan, and she with him. She crouched down, and the cat sat in front of her, mesmerized, as she stroked him with both hands from his face all the way down to his bobbed tail.

Lush cattail reeds grew along the edges of the shimmering lake. The lake acted as a moat around the island of Avalon. There were pink and white apple blossoms growing from the trees in the orchard. The temperature was exactly perfect; it was not warm or cold. The air smelled incredibly sweet and green.

The next thing Sage knew, she was being ushered into Morgan's chambers. *She is not just a magic faerie woman, she must be a princess as well,* Sage thought. Because it seemed that everything Sage's eyes fell upon was exquisitely beautiful—all the things a girl or woman would want to have. There were blue and white china bowls full of pearls, precious gems, and gold. There were rich velvets of purple and green, and piles of lace. There was a box made of bone with engraved gold borders, with a giant ruby inlaid on top; and a looking glass with a hand painted porcelain backing and a carved gold handle. Who was this woman? There was even a small, delicate harp. *How I hope to hear her play that harp,* thought Sage.

The bed in the corner must have been Morgan's because the Lynx leapt right up and actually curled himself on top of the pillow. He was far too big for the pillow and quite squashed it, but he stayed there anyway, and slept. Morgan's face lit up at the sight of him. *I can see that she loves cats,* Sage thought. Morgan looked at her and nodded as she spoke an assent in the Voice. That is when Sage knew that to some degree, Morgan could read her mind. It was something that would have been disturbing, had it been anyone else.

Then Sage's eyes fell upon a deck of cards, lying facedown, on top of a wooden stool near the fireplace. The thick cards had ornate backs of a velvety magenta material that was inlaid with symmetrical patterns of gold. "May I look at your cards?" Sage spoke, in English, to Morgan. She wasn't expecting to. In the instant Sage remembered that Morgan did not speak her language, Morgan said "Yes" in her high and deep vibrating way. So they could understand each other.

Sage sat down on a trunk. Morgan's cards all depicted animals, every one, including birds and some insects. These cards did not have living pictures, as Sage's did. But each animal had a wonderful face, full of wisdom. She remembered Artos' voice from the fortress: 'You must never underestimate the power of animals and the examples set by them.' And she looked at her Lynx. By now Morgan was on the bed with him, petting him, looking quite in heaven. *Yes, I know how good that fur feels,* thought Sage.

Morgan began to speak. The words, if that's what they were, rumbled over one another like rocks moving in a stream. The translation came as this: "He's a Lightning Cat. The word 'Lynx' has its origin in the words 'white' and 'light.' I'm sure you know, he is very wise."

At this Sage felt the now familiar but always awesome quiver of resonance flow through her whole system. It was more than coincidence that Morgan called him a Lightning Cat, and he himself had said: 'Like lightning I will stand by you.'

After looking at them all, Sage shuffled Morgan's animal cards. This was not something one could just do without permission of the owner. But in this case, the feeling was strangely one of "what's mine is yours, and what's yours is mine." She took the shuffled stack and whisked the cards out in the shape of a lightning bolt on the nearest table.

The one she chose had an otter on it. "The otter," she said as she held it up for Morgan to see.

Morgan had an enthusiastic reaction to it. Her warbling translated as: "The otter represents sisterhood and friendship; the message is to be playful, sharing and giving." Then Morgan stood and went to her jewel bowl, with the glittering stones and gold. She came back with an amethyst amulet and reached out, fastening it around Sage's neck. "For you," she uttered, and handed her the looking glass. Sage was stunned by the semi-precious stone. It was a large violet amethyst, in a gold cross-shaped setting. "I thank you, so deeply, Lady."

"Let us go out of doors, Sage."

Morgan left the door ajar, no doubt so the cat could get out. Sage was ecstatic to be back out in the fresh spring air, with the golden sunrays gleaming off of everything in sight, the air sweet and sharp, and the waters of the lake glittering. It was good to be alive! And so magnificent outside, she could not imagine ever desiring to be inside again. Her hand went to her amulet, and she smiled at Morgan like a sister. *We will be best friends, and I finally have a sister,* she thought.

Morgan took her hand, and they walked towards a rather pointy hill, bright green with grass, with horizontal ridges in its side, topped with a ring of tall thin stones. There were seven stones, and Sage thought it looked like a smaller version of Stonehenge. But the power emanating from that circle was anything but small. They walked directly up the hill rather than following the ridges which wound around it.

When they reached the top and were within the stones, Morgan said: "This is the most enchanted of hills in all the land, Sage. Not only is there this sacred crown of stones at the top, but there are secret chambers within. We call it simply, the Tor. "

"I know I have been here," Sage said in a very quiet voice, for she was in honor of the holy ground.

"The stone circle is for services of worship. But I like to just *be* up here," uttered Morgan's sacred tongue.

"Morgan, why did Artos and I have to go to a different time to come here, to see you?"

A sadness that looked just like Artos' crossed over Morgan's face, but stayed longer. "Sage, in the future, from whence you came, this place no longer exists."

Sage's face was puzzled and Morgan continued. "Soon, in not very much time, this most holy of places will be attacked. It will be torched and burned. The stones we stand among right now will be fallen and crushed and reused to build a church for... for..." And then her face wore a most blazing hatred, a hatred that came from all times, past, present, and future. A hatred that actually had validity.

"Why must stupid people destroy that which is wise?!" Morgan demanded of the sky.

"And they won't just destroy—they will steal. And call it their own." Her vexation seemed infinite. Then she regained most of her composure, facing Sage and resuming her incendiary story.

"We know of the Christ. Jesus. He has been here. He was an avatar and the finest magician to ever dwell on the earth. Strangely, though, there is a group who say they follow him, say they follow his word, yet they understand him and his teachings not at all."

"They will renounce our magics. They will call us evil. They reject our ways because we are pagan—meaning polytheistic, we believe in more than one god. They hate women. I wonder, without women, how would they have been born? They say—as if they know—that there is only one god, and if we do not agree to believe in their one god, all will be destroyed of ours, of Avalon. It is close, Sage. I have Seen it."

Sage could not bear to see her new best friend, and sister, in such pain. At once all the recent magics in her life began to charge through her blood and psyche; she heard the Lynx telling her to invent her own magic, that that was her destiny; she heard his growling sounds that said "Like Lightning, I will stand by you," and she said to Morgan:

"Do not worry, sister. I will Bring...Avalon...Back."

Her voice held strong under the mightiness of the words, and in that moment and second, a thin unexpected lightning bolt cracked down from the sky and hit the hill.

"You *will* be avenged. That is my solemn offering."

And the truth, we all know it has a certain ring to it, and it danced like harps across the hill, leaving Sage and Morgan for a moment smiling.

Eight

DOBHRAN'S COUNTRY

"Draw one, Sage, to see what we should do next," Morgan said, in the now familiar rich holy voice.

They were in Morgan's chambers again. The experience on the Tor was so intense in clarity that they did not discuss it. The Lynx was still on Morgan's pillow, and Morgan had just discovered Sage's cards, and was fascinated with them.

Some spring air was wafting through the window, bringing in sweet smells. Sage shuffled and chose, and she held in her hand, again, the card with moss coated rocks and lichen covered trees. The stream inside the card trickled along.

"Oh, you like moss?"

"Yes, lady, it is a thing sacred to me. It is like a soft thick fur upon the earth, and thus I find it soothing."

"Then I know just where we need to go. It is a place of peace and you shall love it."

Sage could not think of a greater place of peace than where they were, but if Morgan said it, it must be so. The Lynx must have read her mind because, as she was thinking she wanted him to come along, he moved. He issued forth a great yawn, whiskers sticking straight out. He stretched mightily, first with his great front paws; then he stood and arched his back. Finally, as he walked towards them along the length of the bed, he extended his hind legs in a stretch, one at a time. He bounded to Sage's feet with a short purring noise, as if to say: "I am ready."

Sage and the Lynx followed Morgan out the door, and they went in a new direction. Something strange was happening. Sage felt like she knew the trees. Their bark was vibrating. Each tree felt like it had its own personality. Then the sky above them changed, and became darker and had a purplish hue to it. She looked back over her shoulder, and saw that the sky over the lake and Morgan's dwelling was much lighter.

"Morgan, are we still in Avalon?"

"Shh—look."

Sage looked and became absorbed. The country was definitely different now, and should have been called *Land of the Holiest*

Moss, she thought. The greenest mosses spread out before them, carpeting the land, and Morgan removed her sandals, gesturing that Sage do the same. The moss under her feet yielded gently, it was so soft and thick, and they walked, padding over it, deeper into this primeval forest. Light came down through the cracks in between treetops, and it was a new shade of light, purplish even more than before. Everything was shades of green and purple, thick disks of lichen clutched the tree bark, and Sage thought she could go on forever, feeling this moss beneath her feet.

"Lady, what is this place." Her voice held awe in it, and as she looked at her cat, he seemed to be almost smiling at her.

"It is the country of the faeries. Now don't be surprised, Sage, because they're going to know you."

And that they did. As small people approached them along the moss trail, they greeted her, calling her "Draigathar." The name sounded vaguely familiar to Sage. They kept saying it, while inclining their heads, sounding surprised to see her. "Draigathar." "Draigathar!"

They are beautiful little people, Sage thought. An unusual light beamed out of their faces. They had rosy red cheeks and bright eyes. Now she really was in an alternate reality. *Please God, let me always feel this feeling of safety.* She was surrounded by great thick evergreen trees with immense boughs, the purplish-green light, and many faerie people. Strangely, she felt not overwhelmed, but instead very relaxed. The place made her feel almost drunk, but in a good way.

"Come to our feasting, Draigathar."

They treated Morgan as a dear friend they saw often. The Lynx stayed right by Sage's side, as if to protect her. In the open area were long tables and rough benches and there were bowls of berries, carafes of mead, and dried meats and fruits and loaves of bread. Ivy and blackberry brambles, growing high above heads, formed a canopy of decoration.

The faeries actually lived within the trees. They chose the wide ones, had hollowed them out, and created living spaces within. Sage could even see miniature flowered curtains through the window openings.

Morgan and Sage and the Lynx sat (the Lynx sat on the ground, at Sage's feet) at the end of a long table, and a faerie man sat across from Sage. *He has kind eyes and is extremely handsome*, Sage thought. He told her his name was Dobhran. His hair was brown and curly and he had brown eyes too. As she looked around her she noticed most of the faerie people had leather clothing.

Dobhran spoke. "You have been gone for a very long time, My Lady." His dialect was similar to Morgan's, it sounded a lot alike, and his own voice was rich and smooth, and she thought she should like to hear it every day. But she was confused about what he said. Morgan was one moment from explaining, but she thought better of it. *Let her enjoy Dobhran's attentions and sweet voice,* she thought.

Dobhran sensed Sage's confusion and it looked like for all the world, there was nothing more he would like to do than explain things to her. "Do you not remember us, Lady? Remember me?"

She was startled. "I am sorry, Dobhran. Something about this place feels familiar, and very safe and secure. But that is all I remember."

He looked saddened, but only for a second, then: "Well at least you are back now. I have been praying for your return." Morgan, like a ghost, silently rose and evaporated into the throng of faeries, into their glee and torches and firelight. But the Lynx stayed and guarded Sage's feet.

Dobhran and Sage were virtually alone now, as many faeries were dancing and playing music. Morgan played upon a harp, and its delicate, eerie strains permeated the purple air. Food smells still lingered, and the evening was balmy warm. Her eyes caught the light of fire from many directions, and the man in front of her gazed upon her as though she was the only woman on earth. Sage was utterly in ecstasy.

"Lady, where have you been?"

"I have been in the future, My Lord." And when she said it she knew two things: she *had* been in the future, and that this was her true home. And she knew that Dobhran was her beloved. "Now, I am starting to remember you." She could not have said something to make him happier, and he reached his hands across the table, strong brown hands, and took hold of hers.

"Draigathar, it has not been good, living without you."

"My Lord, I thought I would never find you again. So much I have forgotten, almost everything, in going to the future." She was remembering though, more and more, mostly remembering their love. She looked at him, right at him, and knew the love that few still believe in.

"Dragon of Air and Lightning, I knew you would fly back to me."

"What mean you, Dragon of Air and Lightning?"

He regarded her in surprise. "Your name. Draigathar. You forgot that also, Lady." Firelight was on her face, and he knew there was no greater beauty. "Destiny has its own mind, does it not?"

"What mean you, My Lord?"

"I mean I would have you by my side, or in front of me, every day, but your destiny has other plans for you."

She had forgotten everything until he said that, forgotten she had a major task in the other world, that of bringing Avalon back. Until he said that, Sage was ready to spend the rest of her life with Dobhran in the faerie country.

"Lady! Do not be saddened!" He had caught the shadow over her face. "I have loved you for ever and will still love you for ever, whether you are here or not."

She still stared at him, saying nothing.

"It is true, my Beloved. I love you in and out of lives, I love you on earth and beyond it. You are never alone from me, from my love."

And she looked at him and knew it was true.

They spent that one night together, barely sleeping at all, for they had much to say to one another. And when they weren't speaking, they were staring, deeply into each other's eyes.

Nine

LETTING GO OF THE LIES

The purplish green fairy country behind them, they were now back in the golden brightness of Avalon. Sage was adjusting her eyes, not yet realizing that it was her mind that needed the most adjusting.

It was hard, getting her out of that country, thought Morgan. And Morgan knew her pain. To love so deeply that love stretches across time and space—and to then have to walk away from it—it takes much discipline. *But love like that always comes back into being,* Morgan reflected.

Sage needed to speak with Artos, and Morgan knew it even more than Sage did. *She must remember her promise to me,* Morgan thought. Now, she spoke: "Sage, let me talk to the Lynx alone. Go down by the waters of the lake until I call you." They were orders, but between Morgan and Sage the comfort level was such that Sage simply heard kind words. She descended to the shore.

"Lynx, you must pull her out of this. Her mind is still in love, back with Dobhran." Between wise ones few words are necessary. The big furry Lynx, his head lifted high, padded down to the shore on his great paws. This time, as he began his feline speech, Sage recognized it right away. He spoke to her in meows and low growls: "True love between a man and a woman is high and great. But it is not so great as the call of your destiny. If it is fulfillment you seek, go to Artos now. Prepare for your great work of magic."

At once the spring wind whipped around her face. She caught the smell of life itself. She looked up the bank towards Morgan, who was out of earshot, but still watching. That princess—that faerie—she glittered her eyes at Sage, awakening in her the magic that had lived there forever.

"Do not be scared of magic, my sister," Morgan's low voice rumbled out. "It has gateways to beauty that neither of us has yet seen. If you want to discover those gateways, or even one of them, now is your time."

Beautiful Morgan strode down to her. The two women stood on the shore of the lake, with the Lynx at Sage's feet. Morgan's shimmering face gazed upon Sage. "I can not do this without you, my sister of the future. It is time for you to dissolve the rest of the lies in your mind."

Sage knew the lies Morgan was speaking of. The ones that said, "You are not a magician, how could a girl like you work such a great, unprecedented magic such that would bring Avalon back?" The lies laughed at her in scorn. But they were lies, after all. Because what else does God want of us, than to be great?

"How do I deconstruct the lies, sister?" Sage asked.

"It is a choice to be great. It is a choice to have majesty. Lady, it lives in all of us, but few can stand the brightness of those flames. Few can stand knowing that those flames live in us. So most people stand sleeping, they seem awake, but they walk asleep and dreaming."

Sage's skin and blood tingled. "This *is* even better than true love. I can feel it coming alive in me—my magic, I mean."

Morgan's kind face looked upon her patiently. Behind Morgan's head, Sage could see apple blossoms hanging in the trees.

"It takes time, the making of a magician," Morgan said. "It is not about learning new things nearly as much as unlearning limiting beliefs. Beliefs that are jail cells for our minds."

Sage smiled at Morgan as if to say, "Please be patient with me." For the lies knew they were goners and were just holding on for dear life. They struggled in Sage's mind, groping for any stronghold. But she wanted to set them free. *Even you, my lies, you deserve freedom, and will be happier that way.* Lies given freedom turn into the truth.

The wind blew and she smelled the smell of Stonehenge. "Morgan. It is time for Artos and the Lynx and me to go back from where we came. There I will make my plan, and you shall have awareness of it as soon as it is ready."

Artos and Sage and the Lynx went to a hidden area behind some big trees. After Artos uttered some incantations, the three evaporated, while Morgan watched.

"Goddess, my dreams are coming true— that Avalon shall forever and ever be alive on earth, and beyond it."

The pressure of astral projection had hurt Sage's ear canals. But what she really did not understand was, why it was practically the same time of day at Stonehenge as when they first left—in fact, it was the *same* day, she was sure. So she asked Artos about it.

"Indeed, it is the same day, Sage. There is no rhyme or reason to time travel, among other things. But you have much to tell me of your doings in Avalon, with Morgan and the faerie people."

She was starving, and told him so. Artos produced stores of cheeses, dried meats, and breads from within the folds of his cloak. *How he fits that all in there,* she wondered.

First, she ate. Her head felt hollow. Her body felt emptied, as if she had to completely fill it again to become whole. Artos sat there on a fallen bluestone (from the semicircle within the trilithons) and mostly drank water. Sage was on the ground, and thankfully it was quite warm. The Lynx was nearby, chewing on a meat piece Artos had given him. He seemed strangely unaffected by the travel. Just looking at him made Sage feel better and more secure.

"Artos, you will have to bear with me. I am drained from this experience, and barely even have memory of it."

Slowly, the life within the rocks around her, and the life within the air and grass seeped into her. She spoke then and told him of everything, of Morgan's chambers and the amethyst amulet (she reached up to her neck, and it was there); of the moss leading into the faerie country; of Dobhran. And she told him about the Tor. It came last, in memory. She recited the events, her eyes staring off into the distance as she spoke, seeing it and feeling it and remembering it as it was.

Now she leveled her eyes at Artos' silvery blue eyed face, the face of kindness and wisdom, and said: "Sir, I know I meant it when I said it, that I would bring Avalon back, and somehow inside of me I know it is the truth. But how..."

The wiseman raised one hand, palm side towards her, for silence. "My young magician, it is sleep that you need, and you need it desperately. You will sleep, covered, for this whole day and night, and the Lynx and I will guard you. Tomorrow, we ride for the fortress at first light. This issue will not be spoken of again till we are within courtyard walls."

And it was done. She sank back in relief and forgetfulness, breathing deeply into her abdomen, until she entered the land where sleep lives.

Without Sage's knowledge of it, her soothsayer friend chanted healing incantations over her head, and blessed her deeply, and called on God to imbue her with courage.

———

They arrived at the fortress quite late the following night. The horses were tired but Sage felt strangely awake. Her lengthy sleep of the preceding day and night had restored her wildness. With a growl to state his departure, the Lynx lumbered off into the woods.

"Shall we speak now, my lord, in the moonlight within the courtyard?" Artos knew this was more so a statement of what was to be, than a request.

"I grant it to you, lady." Rubbing two dry sticks together, he made fire faster than anyone she had ever seen, and with it lit a torch, handing it to her. He tended to the horses, while Sage moved through to the kitchen, lighting candles. She wanted to see if the charcoal cat was on her bed. And behold, as she entered her rose room, there upon the bed was the charcoal gray cat. He was sitting where he was the first time she'd seen him, looking at her with knowing in his eyes. *What is it about this cat? I feel like he is telling me something,* she wondered. The cat's eyes spoke of ancientness and high times.

"Magic lives in everything. It is just for you to see it." Artos' smooth voice permeated the room, and the cat looked up at him in recognition.

"So. Let us go to the courtyard, my lord, where I need to do a card spread." Until this time Sage had been choosing one card at a time. Instinct traveled from her abdomen to her mind now, telling her that this time one card was not enough. "We need a good cloth for this." She glanced around her. There was an ornate brocade tapestry embroidered with blue and gold threads, folded amongst the books. It had such an air of having been loved, she snatched it right up.

They entered the courtyard and by the light of the near full moon, the lichen could be made out on the marble benches. In this light it looked almost white. Sage went directly to the lichen, gently putting her hands on it.

"I am so glad we are back within these walls. They make me feel solid." Then she spread the tapestry on the grass, near the benches. It was as if she had to be as close to the lichen as she could get. "And now Sir, I will shuffle my cards." She closed her eyes and began to concentrate, but Artos interrupted her.

"Sage, before doing that, let me tell you about some Druidic spreads, and you can choose which one..." But he was cut off, because now it was she who gestured for silence.

"My lord, I will make up my own spread. And I will intuit my own interpretations." She looked at the sky. She looked at the moon. She closed her eyelids and pressed her fingers against her eyeballs. Speaking to all of space, she said:

"My heartbeat pulses in my eyes. Great Holy Violet...Dragon's Fire—where is the light?"

He watched as his apprentice with glazed over eyes swirled her cards about, then chose, then laid them out in a row. Then she was running her hands above them, choosing more and laying them over the first row. He could see the path card taking the primary position. Within the card, the leaves on the trees swayed.

She spoke in a language that he had never heard, it sounded almost like coins, metals rubbing against and trinkling over each other. Then he deciphered the words:

"At the end of the path there is a hollow. That's where I live. The treetops make a cave of the end of the road... there is a dog there...do not try, just be..."

"Release me, Lady! Initiate me." She was addressing her own self. Then she snapped the cord on the lies and they floated away and disintegrated.

"It's over, Artos, it's over."

She turned away from the cards, leaving them quivering all over the ground on the tapestry. She settled herself on her bench, feet on the ground, and leaned forward, with her hands flat on the bench on each side of her. He knew she was feeling the lichen.

Ten

INSIDE THE TOR

"So what do I need to know of Avalon?" He was being addressed, and though the long horseback ride was tiresome, Artos now had to speak.

"Of all places to save, it would be the most important. Avalon was a breeding ground for magic. But it was its very awesomeness that brought it down. You see, the people of the new religion, that of the Christ, were intimidated by such great magic. Christ himself was a magician, they just did not understand him. They called magic evil. It was simply their ignorance. But also I think it was their jealousy. They wanted followers for their religion. By renouncing magic and those who practiced it—heretics,

94

they called them—and by preaching fear of God, they slowly but surely turned the people of this land to their way of thinking."

"The greatest irony is, God and fear are exact opposites; they can in no way be equated. By teaching people to fear God, their priests learned to control the masses through guilt. Guilt and doubt took over the mass psyche. It works like that, minds are linked."

"But they could not just reject Avalon, Sage. They torched and burned it, as Morgan described. They brutally killed many wisemen and wisewomen—Druid priests and priestesses. They kill if one does not share their belief in one god. So they kill in the name of God. There is no greater hypocrisy."

Sage was now beginning to understand the hatred she had seen on Morgan's face. She found this information very disturbing. "Artos, we must now stop. It is dreadfully late. And there is the whole day of tomorrow for teaching and learning."

Knowing she was right, he ceased his monologue, and the two entered the stillness of the fortress interior.

———————

"Things disappear when no one believes in them, in their existence, anymore." Artos spoke as birds chirped quietly in nearby trees. It was early morning at the fortress now, and they were out in the cool wet air.

Just barely in the background, they could hear the sea. "It is akin to the dissolution of molecules."

"But what of memory, then, lord? And you yourself said 'minds are linked.' "

"My lady?" He looked inquisitively at her for clarification; it seemed she was combining two different concepts. But the moment she began speaking, it all made sense to him.

"Artos—you've spoken of this mass psychic archetype. As I understand it, it means a belief, a myth, that is shared by an entire people—maybe even all on earth, right? But then we have memory. If an entire people can share a mental myth, they can also share a memory of something that once existed in physical form."

She continued. "You've said there are no boundaries in all of infinity." And then: "The memory of Avalon is stored within the British mind. So if Avalon lives in our psyches, it can be put back on earth. Memory can be pulled to the forefront of minds, thus drawing the molecules back together into form..."

Artos broke in. "It will be hard for people to remember something of which there is no record. Those that destroyed Avalon also destroyed all records of it—for this very purpose. They wanted it to cease having ever been a reality. And, as the centuries have passed, in the minds of men Avalon has turned into a myth rather than a real place that once existed."

But Sage wasn't paying attention. She was thinking of the last thing she said: *Memory can be pulled to the forefront of minds, thus drawing the molecules back together into form...*

"I will need to be going to the dragon lines, sir." Unsmiling, she said it in her deep voice, and though the air was warm with spring, he heard that almost cold sound—the subtle, esoteric tone of a wisewoman with magic in her mind.

———

It was inconvenient, as it were; they had just returned to the fortress. But magic has its own call, and when it calls, one must respond. Luckily the place where they were going was much closer than Stonehenge. As they were packing the horses, the Lynx emerged from out of the woods next to the fortress. "Oh Lynx, I am so pleased you are back," Sage said happily. "We must now go to Glastonbury."

Glastonbury! Artos almost coughed in shock. He had thought she wanted to go somewhere else. *She'll have an unpleasant surprise when she sees the Tor,* he thought.

They rode for two hours. Spring pulsed in the buds of bushes and trees. Early leaves were forming. There was that pale, pale green smell that only spring creates.

"I do believe I can actually *see* the bushes growing, Artos."

He had no doubt that she could.

The Tor being so conical in a relative flatland, Artos knew it would not be long before he heard her surprise at what lay there now.

At first she squinted her eyes at the sight, and as they rode closer and closer—it became unmistakable to her. "There's some dratted church tower there now, not the ring of stones." As she said the last she remembered: of course there would be no ring of stones. And she remembered Morgan telling her of the church. "But I did not think it would be on the very top of the Tor!"

Indeed, St. Michael's tower looked out of scale. The sight of it kindled an irritation within Sage that slowly turned into flames. It was a strange combination. Spring was glistening in the land, beauty abounded every which way, and within that gentle greenness Sage was angry.

Cat utterances issued from the Lynx at this time, and they turned into words in her mind. He said: "Strength is to be found in following your instinct. Do not bleed off power in anger."

Trust in the Lynx, in his wisdom and his love for her, made her know that truly, being angry would not help her purpose.

"Artos, I must go inside of the Tor. Morgan says there are secret chambers in there." He knew better than to debate with one so certain. By now they were within the trees at the base of the Tor. Sage glanced around, straining her eyes in the direction of the faerie country. She walked toward it. *I wonder if Dobhran is near,* she thought. Briefly she thought of their love. And then she remembered her destiny.

Artos tied the horses to the trees. He turned to see Sage and the Lynx coming out of a stand of white birch trees. She floated. She moved like she didn't have feet, only the flowing folds at the base of her gown. "I have no more blood in me, Lord. It is only lightning."

Artos began realizing that Sage was not completely human. Her eyes became glazed over and glimmery and he thought how like a dragon she looked. Those eyes in their greenness looked at him, right in his pupils, and she spoke:

"I speak to the blackness
of the pupil
in your eye,
the blackness that is
all of space
and all of eternity."

For a few moments the spring world became dark as if under a purple haze. Sage breathed deeply and felt new crevices in the depths of her lungs open up to accommodate the air.

"Breathe of this magic air, my lord. It contains the Holy Violet Flame." Then:

"Lightning lives in me, Artos. I have always known it, but until now I did not have the strength to let it flow through."

She stretched her hands high above her head until her arms were completely extended. Her mouth formed into a scream, but there was no sound. Then: "They are waiting for me. The Lynx and I must go alone—I don't know why." She bowed to Artos as a gesture of departure.

Sage blinked at the sight of a door in the side of the Tor that one second ago had not been there. It was dark gray iron with cast curving patterns and it seemed to be behind a mist, and definitely looked like it would disappear at any second. "Lynx, through this door!" As she leaned forward to grasp the ancient knob, the door swayed open towards her, and she pulled it, letting the cat precede her. Then she darted through.

Inside it was so much brighter than Sage expected. It was not just the fires and torches. There was light emanating from the walls and ceiling, which were all stone, but she could not determine its source. The Lynx stood right at Sage's side.

Then a man came out from around a corner. He looked rather like Artos, but much older. He was silvery and handsome and beautiful with long white hair and blazing blue eyes. He wore a long blue tunic. Sage knew it was Merlin, before he said anything.

He bowed to her. "So long, so long it has been, Draigathar. I did not know you would be bringing such a beautiful cat." And the Lynx allowed himself to be petted by the man.

Sage wanted to embrace Merlin. She was remembering again, as she had remembered in the faerie country. Merlin was regarding her with the kindest of eyes. "My young friend, it must have been very difficult for you to get here. We have all been sending you messages for many years."

Sage kept listening to him talk, as it was that rippling language, like rocks tumbling downstream. Like Morgan's. With no effort her mind translated it. She loved the sound of it. "My Lord Merlin, what language is it that you speak?"

"It is called Ogham, a sacred Druid tongue. If you would, lady, there is someone I would have you meet." She and the Lynx followed him around the corner from where he had come, into a deeper chamber. It was blue-ish in here, not as bright. But the person sitting alone in the room, on a stone bench, was very bright. Glowing, in fact. Sage doubted he was completely human. She looked in his eyes and crumbled to the floor on a leopard skin. His eyes were golden. Infinite love poured from them, into Sage.

"Draigathar, this is Jesus. Jesus the Christ."

The whole room was full of the love that poured out of His holy eyes. When she breathed in, the love went into her lungs. Now she knew where her lightning came from. It came from Him.

It was so quiet, so quiet now. The Lynx had come and laid down next to Sage on the leopard skin. The Lynx looked at the Christ also. Cat and God stared at each other. Jesus smiled at the Lynx. Sage rested one hand on his thick soft fur. She gathered her courage and looked up to see Jesus' eyes again. His eyes could look in all directions at once, including into hers. He spoke truth to her with those endless eyes, and his mouth never opened. The deepest peace engulfed her. When she looked in His eyes her mind ceased to exist. She became him, became absorbed by him. Anything that had ever seemed like a problem disintegrated.

Eleven

BRINGING AVALON BACK

Merlin had not been present during Sage's encounter with Jesus. He had not wanted to distract her in any way. Sage had fallen asleep upon the leopard skin, and when Merlin entered, Jesus was gone, though the glow of his love still hung in the air. Merlin placed a warm blanket on top of Sage's body, though the Lynx was sleeping right up against her. There he left her, and he went back to study while he waited for her to awaken.

It was the Lynx who woke Sage up. His enormous forepaws were pushing into her back, thus bringing her back from the land of sleep. She reached behind herself, petting him. There was a small fire in the cave-like room and she opened her eyes to that. The flames cracked and hissed as she pulled her body into a sitting position. "Lynxy." She stroked him lovingly. *What would I do without this cat?* She wondered. Sage stared into the flames and remembered everything that happened with Jesus. She had never felt so calm.

She groped about for her card pouch. She removed the entire deck from the pouch, gently touching the cards, including their purple backs with the lightning bolts and cat's paw prints. She leafed through them, in utter fascination. Waters churned and sprayed in the sea. Trees bent softly in the wind. The bird was in flight. In the thunder and lightning card, little lightning bolts were cracking down. It was all before her: fire, risk, light, faith. Silence, freedom, instinct, destiny.

And a voice spoke inside of her mind: "Each card reflects a facet of your own internal wisdom. You already know everything. These cards are mirrors of the wisdom that lives inside of you. I remind you of who you are through the cards." Sage knew it was the Goddess.

She then formed the cards back into a deck and shuffled gently. She did not want to hurt any of the pictures or the animals that lived inside of them. When it was time to cut the deck and draw, two cards pulled at her. She turned them over. The great wild cat. The castle. *What had Artos said?* The cat represents freedom, wildness, detachment. And the castle? Elegance, success, maturity, manifestation. She gazed into the beauty of the cards. Colorful flags waved in the wind from the battlements and towers of the castle. The cat's eyes were old and deep and she knew it was alive. *I know that ancientness. It lives in my very own soul.*

She thought, *I am more within the magic vein than ever. Now would be a good time to enter.* She stared into the wildcat's eyes and uttered "Parasamgate."

No one was there to look within the card, and see Sage's transparent ghost sitting near the wildcat. But the Lynx, as always, guarded her physical body.

Sage beheld the orange wildcat in front of her. He had brown markings and yellow eyes and a very wide, thick tail that puffed out at the end. The cat exuded a warrior spirit. That is to say, he seemed almost on the offense. But then he purred at her, loudly, and this is what the purring meant:

"There is no one true reality. Always be wild, Lady. Always be free. Move about within the worlds, enlightening people and places as you go. Be detached; you will have more power that way."

Sage reached out to touch the wildcat's thick orange coat. He allowed her to do it, but she could tell this was not a cat accustomed to humans, or human ghosts, for that matter. Again he began his speech:

"Lightbearers come in many forms—some are human, some animals, some plants, stars, stones."

Then: "I can point the way to that castle, the one you want to attend next."

Astonished, but only for one moment, Sage realized he meant the castle within the card she had just chosen. Lifting a thickly padded paw, the cat gestured towards the east. Sage could just make out the colored flags, waving in the wind from the towers and battlements. *It is the same castle!* she thought.

"Come, I will guide you." The cat set off towards the castle, and Sage had to be quite spry to keep up with him.

"O Cat, is there a name for this country?"

"We are in the Caledonian Highlands, Lady," he purred.

They traversed huge rocks, small hills, and fallen timber as they wound amongst giant trees and glistening lakes. Flowers Sage had never seen in her life, purple and yellow, graced the land. They crept closer to the castle. It was quite ornate and complex. She could not even count all the turrets and conical roofed towers, and it became clear that the castle was rambling all over atop a hill. Each window was framed with an arched molding, and there were many dormers and parapets and spires.

The wildcat hadn't meant to, but he had taken to Sage. He was a true cat, very aloof, for he had seen the pain that comes with attachment, be it to another animal or a place. But he liked this girl. He puffed up his fur, and it was very orange, and he strutted along. Sage could not help but like this cat. He had elegance about him, like the lord of a manor.

Nearing the castle, it suddenly occurred to Sage that she did not know what to do. To whom should she speak, or should she speak at all? In fact, *could* she speak? She was but an apparition. What to do? She did not wish to alarm any castle dwellers. So she decided to find a secluded low hill upon which to perch, and view the castle from a short distance.

Sage and the orange wildcat hunkered down next to a bush on a sheltered hill, where she was sure they would not be seen. Mature trees provided shade from the sun. The inner workings of her intuition took over. The cat not being the chatting type, they ceased any conversation. She gazed upon the stone castle. The inner workings of her intuition caused her to be most interested in the very stones themselves. And she began to think about stone. She heard Artos' voice: "Rocks symbolize acceptance. They readily accept snow, rain, sun and all variations of the above without changing."

A transmutation began occurring within her psyche. She stared at the large stones of the castle again. They each sat, in their places, in a silent meditation. Even with the season's extreme temperature changes, the molecules that comprised stone were not malleable. *The way my core is not malleable,* she thought. And then she knew that she *would* do anything to bring Avalon back; that this desire was in her core and it could not be changed, like stone.

She stared long at the castle, marveling. No one had shouted out answers from the castle towers. Just staring at the beauty of the castle and at its individual stones had caused her to be aware of her own enlightenment and wisdom, just as the Goddess had said. Sage heard the orange wildcat's purring voice in her memory: "Always be wild, Lady. Always be free." And with that inspiring memory she leapt up, scampering down the hill, her ghostly legs taking her to the nearest lake. As she plunged in, for the first time she felt what it was like, to be a ghost in water.

The orange wildcat looked on, for he had followed. Sage was beyond waterproof; the water glimmering with sunlight poured right through her amorphous body, her green eyes the only solid things he could see.

Sage's spirit re-entered her physical body just a few moments before Merlin entered the room. There she was, still lying upon the leopard skin. She remembered everything that had happened with the cat and castle, but there was no need to mention it to Merlin. Instead, she asked him something else:

"Sir, from where hails this leopard skin?" She asked because, it did not seem right or possible that one of Merlin or Jesus' nobility would kill a leopard, and show off the pelt. The fur was thick and soft, and though she adored its beauty, it hurt her to wonder about the end of the leopard who wore it.

Merlin got a far-off look upon his face. Beneath a thin layer of sadness, Sage could see great joy. "He was my leopard, a snow leopard at that. You see how the base fur is almost white? At one time in my training I lived far to the east of these lands. Very far. I lived in mountainous snow country. Can you imagine the glory of seeing an animal with that kind of fur, traversing the land, right near your own dwelling? Majesty. Those cats are kings. But this one, he was closest to me, and he had a big heart and mellifluous eyes. And the tail on him! The tail alone weighed nearly as much as the rest of him! He lived to be very old, Sage, for a snow leopard, and on his dying day, he said: 'Sir, in the future I will barely exist, there will be so few of my kind. And earth's people will mourn my demise. But know this: Now is the height of my proliferation, I am abundant, and this time is part of the Oneness of the Holy Now. So this time lives forever. Do not miss me in the future. I am here, always.'

"And so I kept his fur. To remind me of him, and of the Holy Now."

They sat in silence for a moment, Sage imagining the scene Merlin had described.

"Do you understand, Sage? Time is one totality encapsulated in a vast Now."

"I do not know why, but I do understand, Merlin." It made her happy to think that his words were true.

Then she had a request. "Merlin, if you would, I truly need to be out of doors. I do not know or care what time of day or night it is, I do not know if the sun is shining or if it is raining, but indeed I do need fresh live air."

"Desire granted, lady." She stood to follow him, but as he left the room she had to stop and look back. It was hard to walk away from the room where she met Jesus. She wondered how long the love would last in the room. "I will be needing to leave some of my blood here, Merlin." So saying she pierced her wrist with a dagger, and with her thumb she squeezed blood out onto the stone of the hearth.

"Now it will be near to the fire."

Her blood was different than human blood, it was still red, but it emitted a vibration of incandescent wildness that Merlin could not ignore.

They went out the same dark gray iron door with cast curving patterns. It was dark outside, and it was raining. Immediately Sage went into a cluster of trees to use as a latrine. The Lynx followed her and did the same. The gentle pattering of raindrops on leaves was as soothing as anything had ever been.

When she and the cat emerged Merlin led her to an enclosure made of gnarled tree branches. There were two benches and a little table. They sat on the benches and looked through the open doorway as the raindrops continued to fall. The Tor was right nearby and they could see it through the doorway. It was quite warm, and Sage could smell apple blossoms. Merlin offered her Chalice Well water and dried fruit pieces. The Lynx rubbed against Sage's leg, and she knew it was time that he would be off. They were not home and she did not want to lose him. She leaned over and looked at his handsome face, saying, "Do not go far, Lynx. Come back to me soon." He knew what she said and strode out of the shelter, out for a night of stalking.

Merlin's blue eyes blazed in the otherwise dim surroundings. She spoke: "His eyes are like endless tunnels, lord." And then: "I know Him and I've known Him forever." Merlin knew she was speaking of Jesus.

Then Merlin spoke. "That is because He lives in us." For a moment a violet haze surrounded Merlin's body and head, then gradually faded. "This is your Initiation to Freedom, Draigathar. Freedom from fear. Freedom from doubt. Freedom is magic, and magic is free."

She considered his words, and the cat card came to mind, causing her spine to tingle. She said, "Jesus's love bestowed freedom upon my mind."

In the far off distance they could make out the rumble of thunder. "How auspicious," said Merlin quietly.

Sage spoke. "The thunder is the most truth I've heard spoken. It drowns uncertainty. It cracks my brain wide open with the voice of God."

She dashed outside and Merlin followed. She stood facing the Tor. Her hair whipped wildly around her. In the end it settled like a mane, framing her face. *She is wild,* thought Merlin.

"Merlin, I feel like all the magicians are inside of me. All the magicians of the world distilled their magic and have sent it coursing through my veins." Her pupils were dilated and white light like stars emanated from their centers. She continued:

"It feels like the past is speaking to me, Avalon is speaking to me and it wants to come out, it wants to come back and it knows I believe in it. Avalon *is* still alive and existing, it is just barely on the fringes of this reality." Then:

"I do not believe in the limits of the mind."

For a moment she was Medusa with a crown of writhing snakes on her head.

For a moment her feet lifted and she levitated a foot above the ground.

For a moment she grew fangs and claws.

And then she was chanting.

"Forget, forget everything, forget everything..."

"Is there any music that sustains the vibration of magic over and over? I must hear it." It was a command to the inside of her mind. Then she heard harps playing inside of her head, and her heart beat in her brain like drums.

With eyes closed she uttered an incantation, and to whom she spoke, at first Merlin did not know. Then he knew she was speaking directly to Avalon itself:

"A thread connects us,
fine as spider web.
This thread exists only now,
In the pristine gem of the present.
This thread exists nowhere else
For me to feel it—
for me to travel feeling across it
like a tightrope
I must be alive, awake
I must be conscious
Walking the vista of this eternal moment.

I connect with you
in this one instant among trillions
and this instant lasts forever.
Now there is no distance
Now there is no space.
Your country lies on the inside
of my eyelids
You stalk me.

My spine stands straight,
and even in this early morning chill,
I feel you.
I feel you here,
within the holy now."

The wind picked up, lashing her hair in speech. And in that moment and second, a thick unexpected lightning bolt cracked down from the sky and hit the hill. It caused the church to crumble, including the tall tower. The sound of rock scraping rock was like thunder. But it was thundering anyway, and the combination of sounds fed Sage's soul.

She spoke. "I have awakened the spark, the seed of the memory of Avalon. My memory is the catalyst for mass memory. Thus remembrance will begin, and we will see little bits and pieces...of Avalon...this is about one mind consciousness. If I have this memory, this magic and fire in my mind, then everybody has it. I have lit the flame and now it can travel across minds."

There was something different about her voice; it sounded almost pulled from somewhere else, like from a different time.

"There is only one Now, Merlin."

———

And behold, as the days went by, sights of Avalon were visible to some. To most people, it simply looked like the church tower on the

Tor was gone forever. But to some, it seemed that at certain times of the day they could almost see a ring of stones, as it had been centuries and centuries before.

Sage's head hurt, and when she awoke she did not have the slightest inkling where she was, and was eternally grateful to hear the Lynx purring loudly beside her. Why would she know where she was? Of late the young girl had been everywhere, it seemed, in and out of time and space.

Then a brown haired head hovered above her, and she saw Morgan's face, Morgan, her beautiful faerie sister.

They were in Morgan's chamber. Sage looked around her, at Morgan, the Lynx, the fire. The harp, her bright card pouch. Everything seemed so still. Something was different, but she did not know what it was.

"Morgan. What has happened?"

"You pulled it through time, my sister, and through the minds of men. You dragged the memory of it right into the present."

Sage's own memory now was very weak. She did not remember yet, and kept looking at Morgan questioningly.

"Merlin heard it, he heard you, you spoke to Avalon itself. And at the end of your incantation, lightning struck the Tor, bringing down the church."

"Do you mean that Avalon is back in the world?!" At this Sage seemed to have more energy.

"Yes my sweet, you were the vessel that was chosen. Because you believe in infinite freedom, Sage. That is your magic. And that type of freedom has no ceiling, no end, no boundary."

The Lynx purred and purred. Morgan came and sat on the bed, and they petted the Lynx together. Sage suddenly reached up to her throat, feeling for the amethyst amulet. It was still there.

Sage felt it as she spoke. "Now I have done all this work, lady, may I go back and see Dobhran?"

Morgan smiled. "You are asking me? You, My Lady, may do anything that you choose, forever and for all of time."

"Yes, I do want to see Dobhran. But I think, right now, I will sleep again." And she wrapped her arm around the Lynx, and was asleep before her eyelids had completely closed.

Twelve

PATH TO ETERNITY

The Goddess had told Morgan in dreams that this girl would come (Sage). The Goddess told Morgan that Sage still needed much training in unveiling the mind. Sage was to be one of the greatest magicians to ever live. She was to be capable of opening doorways in the mind heretofore closed. Sage had awareness of universal mind consciousness, something so great to bear, that most magician's psyches would crumble under its weight.

But she needs a respite, Morgan mused. She would call on Sage soon, but not yet. As Sage learned the Cards of the Chalice, Morgan would have her teach others.

Sage was itching to see Dobhran. But she had to talk to Artos first. He was in Avalon;

he had been waiting for her to wake up. Now she was awake, he said, "You will be happy to know, lady, that we do not have to travel through time to go back to the fortress."

This shocked her, but after thinking, it made sense. Yes, Avalon was in the present, as was the fortress. She was eternally glad not to endure time travel again any time soon.

They were down by the lake. Morgan and the Lynx sat together, listening to their talk. "Artos, I could smell apple blossoms—Merlin and I were in the shelter—and I could smell the blossoms of Avalon right before I spoke the words that brought it back."

"You brought Avalon back, Sage, not just words."

"We all have brought it back, do you see? I mean, all the magicians of all times were inside of me when I did it, and I was instilled with the love and lightning of Jesus." Artos' eyes got wide, and it dawned upon Sage that once she walked through that mist shrouded door in the side of the Tor, Artos knew nothing of what had befallen her. She told him then, everything. By the shore of the holy lake, which acts as a moat around Avalon, she told him. Of Merlin, and Jesus. Of the orange wildcat and the castle. Of the Goddess speaking inside of her mind. And the magic that traveled through her veins and racked her body to her very core.

"Then it has come to pass that truly you are a Super Cat," said Artos. Morgan looked

quizzical and he explained to her about Sage's surname, Uberchat. Morgan smiled at the sound of the whimsical name, thinking it appropriate.

They all enjoyed the warmth of the sun glinting off the lake. Artos spoke. "Sage, I have news of your town. It seems that—I am sorry to have to announce this. Your father is dead."

At first Sage stared for long moments into Artos' face and eyes. He could see her mind moving. "But...my mother and my brothers, are they all right?"

"They are fine—the tragedy befell your father alone."

A great lifting occurred within Sage. The death of her father felt like a piece of freedom, as though his dying erased his tortures and cruelties. And it did. Relief washed over her like rain. Her mother and brothers now would have relief also. *I will go to them,* she thought. *After I see Dobhran.*

"I thank you for telling me this news, Artos. And now I must go. For the future, it is my intention to go in and out of the faerie country, and in and out of Avalon. I must see Morgan and Dobhran as much as possible. But I will also come and go at the fortress." Her green eyes smiled as she spoke. "I thank you, Artos, for all you have given me, for all you have taught me and for everywhere you have taken me. You are a noble friend."

She now looked upon Morgan, and for some reason did not feel she should say goodbye. The two wisewomen embraced, and then Morgan said: "Go to him! You are in love, and it is true love—why should it wait?"

Sage stepped away, still holding Morgan's hand. She looked at Morgan with sisterly love in her eyes. She thought of her cards. She had only just begun learning how to use them. But right now she wanted to hear her inner voice all by herself. "Morgan, will you safeguard the Cards of the Chalice for me? I do not think I will be needing them in the faerie country."

Morgan nodded as she stared into Sage's green eyes. "I will see you soon, sister."

"Lynx, let us go." They departed, Sage and the Lynx, and headed towards the path of thickest green moss and giant oak trees. Where the light took on a purplish hue. They walked alone amongst the trees, taking care not to trip over rocks, and Sage remembered, then, to remove her boots. Warmth from the earth came up through the moss, and for bare feet there was no better feeling.

She left her boots behind her. She left everything behind her. The woman who walked down that path was blank in the mind. It was her heartbeat that she could feel, and her core with its instinct.

The trees emanated an ancient power, and their roots extended down into sacred ground. This country had never been touched, and never could be, because only those wise could enter. Now her mind held no lies, she could see clearly, and she could see vibrations in the air. She could see the life of the trees, the life of the moss, as it pulsed all around her.

Dobhran came down the path towards them. He was so handsome, and then his mouth was by her ear as he embraced her. "Draigathar." The warm air from his mouth went over her ear and onto her neck, and it kindled in her ancient flames. The peace that she felt at the sight of him, at the touch and feel of him, was the deepest she had ever known.

Man and woman and cat walked into the depths of the forest. She was home.

Segment Two:
Dark Star

One

ENTER DARK STAR

For Dark Star to drink, it was necessary for her to place her front paws on either side of the chalice, and lift it to her human lips. The appearance of Dark Star was a mighty sight to behold: She was mostly human, except that she had leopard paws instead of hands, and leopard hind paws instead of feet. Dark Star's hair was dark, and long, and she had a big black tattoo in the shape of a diamond star centered on her forehead. Beneath her forehead rested her soothing sacred eyes.

She had black tattoos on her arms and wrists, they were dragons, and they ended right where the leopard fur began. Her whole neck was tattooed a continuous Celtic knot. She wore a thin gold crown around her head, encrusted with emeralds. It skimmed over the center of her forehead tattoo, and became one with it: emeralds upon ink. Black velvet robes were her dress preference, but one could always see her spotted leopard feet sticking out the bottom.

The first sign to Morgan that Dark Star had arrived in Avalon was the imprint of her paws in the mud. Morgan noticed it one day as she walked the grounds, and was initially startled. She had been walking back to her dwelling along the old faerie path, and saw the trail of two feline pawprints. Schooled in reading tracks, what Morgan could not understand was why the tracks were only of *hind* feet.

That same night the being that Morgan would learn to address as "Dark Star" arrived on her threshold requesting an audience. Morgan had been sitting by her fire, staring into the flames, when her attendant priestess had come in to announce a visitor.

"Your Majesty.....it is..... *Dark Star*," announced the maiden, very slowly, and she bowed. In uttering these words, the attendant felt as if she had delivered a magic spell. Morgan's head flew up, and she gazed upon Dark Star's prodigious countenance. And her eyes fell to the spotted paws, upper and lower. For a moment, her gaze rested upon the diamond forehead tattoo. Again she met Dark Star's eyes. In her eyes Morgan saw a place higher than laughter, a place beyond ecstasy. Dark Star was swathed in a cloak of solemnity. There was this most ancient silence that surrounded her. It was the quietness from which religions are born.

It felt to Morgan as if all of the problems of the world had disintegrated. Dark Star had glided into the room and glanced, and everything had fallen silent, even the flames. Finally, she opened her human mouth, and she spoke. She had a human voice, but it must be said that the voice had a trace of cat in it; somehow it was feline, as if she was purring as she spoke: "Lady Morgan, I live in the magic inversion. It is where paradox folds back in upon itself. It is the crossover point of infinity, where Now encompasses all of time." So saying, her eyes glittered at Morgan.

Morgan returned Dark Star's gaze. "From where have you come, Lady? I have heard tales of you, but knew not if I would make your acquaintance in this lifetime."

Dark Star understood Morgan's language. "I have ventured from Caithness, Majesty. It is a long journey upon these feet," and with a forepaw she gestured towards the floor, where the spotted fur could be seen poking out from beneath her black velvet folds. "I am of the clan MacLeod. I have seen the future in dreams, and I see that you are in need of assistance. We have a great work before us, yes?" Dark Star's solemnity encompassed her, encompassed both of them. The purring sound of Dark Star's cat voice, Morgan's guttural deep tone, and the snapping of apple tree twigs in the fire, mixed with wind...magic was afoot.

In answer to Dark Star's question, Morgan explained everything, about Avalon and Sage, Sage's work and what they had accomplished so far. She explained how important it was to keep Avalon alive in the world. "For without magic, Lady, what would life be? I understand that in the distant future, humanity has become quite devoid of magic. And so they are suffering greatly. Here is an example: if humans from the future saw you, they would not even see your paws. Their minds are so closed, and programmed so strictly, that anything unusual is invisible to them."

Dark Star was proud of her paws and loved them very much, and they were so real and such a part of her, that Morgan's words had their effect. She purred, "We must at all times remember the core of magic: that everything is possible." She smiled upon Morgan, and they both felt the wind lash at the house, in agreement.

Sage had come back from the faerie country after a few months, to see Morgan. When she knocked on the door of Morgan's dwelling, a most hallowed soul answered the door. It was Dark Star. Sage had never seen her before, nor had she heard of her. Dark Star regally ushered Sage to sit by the fire. As she gestured towards an ornately embroidered bench, the undeniable paw of a leopard was distinctly visible, and Sage gasped.

At the sound of this gasp, Dark Star issued forth a low chortle. "Ah, my daughter, I am of the Scottish cat people, the Kati." She drew breath, staring at Sage, who gratefully sank to the silk cushion of her seat. Sage's eyes were wide, engulfing the tattoos, the paws, the emeralds. A feeling akin to the meeting of Jesus entered her.

"I was born to a half cat, a half leopard. The human gene was strong, though, therefore you see only my paws, front and hind, are of the leopard." So saying she extended her foot to display the furry spotted leopard paw emerging from the folds of velvet. When Morgan burst through the door moments later, Sage looked upon her almost as if she had forgotten Morgan existed.

Morgan appeared amused. "Ah yes, Lady, I see that you have swooned another. Such is the allure of Dark Star." Sage looked from Morgan to Dark Star. This was the first time she had heard her name, and it fell upon her ears as gemstones upon velvet. She thought it was a perfect name for a sublime being. Morgan then approached her. "Sister," she murmured, and they embraced. Sage smelled Morgan's scent of lavender. As their bodies pulled slowly apart, Sage looked into Morgan's eyes and was full of joy and remembering.

Morgan looked to Dark Star. "Have you yet told her why you are here?" she asked with ease and familiarity. Dark Star purred: "My dear, we have only just met—in fact—a proper introduction, by you, is in order."

Morgan straightened her spine, and her hair stood higher upon her head. She gestured for Sage to stand. Morgan began uttering in the Voice. "By the light and warmth of this fire, and by the glow of the fire from the sun, I, Morgan of the Faeries, introduce Dark Star MacLeod of Caithness to Sage Uberchat."

The sound of Sage's name, uttered in Morgan's language and haunting voice, had unusual force and power, which struck Sage to her core. Sage and Dark Star now approached each other and clasped hands and paws, their eyes meeting in an ocular embrace. Sage was elevated to the sacred recesses of Dark Star's world as she stared into that woman's eternal eyes. And her leopard paws felt so warm and soft in Sage's hands.

The spell of the moment hung in the air. Then, a guttural purring growling sound issued from outside. At the sound Morgan's face lit up, and her eyes became wide as she smiled and went to the door to admit the Lynx. "Here, boy," Sage spoke softly to him, patting her thigh. The lush cat walked in, and advanced directly to Sage and rubbed his body against her leg, purring, all the while staring at the new lady. Morgan stroked his back, where his fur was like the thickest of carpets.

Dark Star crouched down to be at eye level with the Lynx. *He is gorgeous,* she thought. The Lynx, mesmerized, approached Dark Star without the slightest hesitation. As she held out a paw, he sniffed it vehemently, alternating his gaze between the leopard's paw and the face of a human. Dark Star petted him too, but it is quite a different experience when done with a paw.

The Lynx, purring loudly, stalked off to find Morgan's bed, where he curled himself upon her pillow. And then he did that miraculous thing that cats do: he purred and slept simultaneously. With the sound of low purring in the background, and the hiss and crackle of the fire in the foreground, a meeting began to take place. Dark Star was seated upon a low, padded bench. She extended her spotted paws before her to raise a chalice of red wine to her lips. The pads on the undersides of her paws were good for gripping. She had been drinking this way all of her life.

She glanced at her colleagues. "Morgan, Sage, we must commence work. I have seen the distant future, and in the minds of most men Avalon is still lost to the world. It must be made more tangible. Those with the magic bone must be able to enter. Sage was sent to the future, roughly five hundred years hence, to bring Avalon back, and it worked! But it is still not tangible enough to extend further into the future." She looked at Sage. "Do not for one moment think I am minimizing your extraordinary feat, Sage. What you have already created is the beginning of the savior of Avalon. I am simply impressing upon both of you this: in the distant future, Avalon is crying out to be heard. And that is why we are here right now. That is why we are having this discussion."

As no words escaped the lips of Morgan and Sage—they just stared at her—Dark Star continued. "I am prepared to reign in Avalon. Morgan has worked long and hard here. Certainly she will be right next to me, but I am willing to take charge." What looked like relief on Morgan's face was exactly that, this being perhaps even an understatement. A mighty project was being proposed, and Morgan was all too happy to relinquish her control to that of another, especially one so noble as Dark Star. "So here is what I propose. We must commune with that future. The beings of that future are starved of their inherent magic. Their inherent magic is shrouded by thick layers of deception, some as old as millennia."

"We must project ourselves, our power and magic and force, into the future where there is a connecting point waiting, wanting to receive us. She is mostly a human being; her name is Axis. Axis carries the gene of faerie. That is why she is able to hear us. She has answered my repeated call, which I have made through prayer, hope, and faith. My call has been silent, but she responds to silence. Axis exists one thousand five hundred years hence towards the future. She needs our help as much as we need hers. You see, Axis is trying to bring Avalon back into that time—into that reality—very desperately. Most humans of her time believe that it was never even real—only a legend! But Axis believes in us, in Avalon."

Sage spoke, "Lady—wait—how do we communicate with this being, this...Axis?" Dark Star considered the question, and then responded. "I came to her as a hawk and left her feathers. Now she can smell me. It is my most tangible connection with her as of yet." Still, Morgan looked a trifle puzzled. "Lady..."

Dark Star interrupted her. "Axis used to live in Avalon when it was alive and thriving. But since her soul is in a different incarnation now, her memory of Avalon is very cloudy and blurry. We must do everything to remind her that it is *real.*"

Morgan burst in with her thoughts: "Do you hear what you are saying, Dark Star. You say Axis used to live here when it was alive. That is happening now—from where we sit, Avalon is still alive! That means Axis's soul incarnation might be here *now*. If she is here, we must discover which maiden she is. Was. Is."

Slow smiles crept onto their faces. Sage felt a chill run up her spine and Dark Star got goosebumps. "This is a magic transaction. Something is afoot."

Two

THE ASSEMBLY OF DISCOVERY

"What did you mean about her carrying the gene of faerie?"

They were sitting on the Tor, amongst the seven megaliths—the same circle within which Sage told Morgan she would bring Avalon back.

This question was directed at Dark Star by Sage. During the steep walk up the Tor, Sage had been wondering about it. *How could a human be only part faerie?*

"It's quite simple really. The same way I have cat blood, born to a half cat, Axis descends from faeries. As the centuries have trickled along, the faerie blood has been diluted, of course. But! Axis is so keen to know all, about her self, her past, about

Avalon, that she discovered it all by herself from her inner guidance: that she indeed carries faerie blood."

The sun could barely be seen, though the sky was warm and gold and the mossy ground upon which they sat was an agreeable temperature. Sage sat on the earth cross legged, digging about in a clover patch, attempting to find a four leafed specimen.

"So you are thinking that Axis's soul counterpart, as it were, is here right now, in Avalon? Morgan is right, we must discover who. But how?" She asked the last question of herself, more than anything. "Wait! I've hit upon something!" With her brow furrowed, Sage continued: "We could call an assembly. Be straight with the maidens. Tell them all. Then, everyone, including us, would be required to go into a say, twenty four hour silent meditation. Each and every one of us would ask our innermost wisdom: *Who is it? Is it myself, even?* And by the end of twenty four hours, Morgan, Dark Star, I do believe we'd hit upon the answer."

It was a sound idea, perfect in fact, and Morgan set about arranging it.

———

Avalon's room of assembly was not so large, for generally there were about twenty-five maiden priestesses in training. All were present. Flaming torches lined the walls, and up front on the dais, sat Morgan. Fluttering, hushed voices created a low din, until Morgan, schooled in the language of gesture, raised a single hand in such a manner that silenced them.

"Maidens, becoming deeply calm will serve you, and Avalon, the most at this time. As you are aware, Avalon will be attacked, and displaced from the world, in the very close future. It will hang on by a thread on the outermost edges of linear reality. It will cease to be a center for the training of magic." These heavy words descended upon the ears of the maidens and not a twitter was heard.

At this time Dark Star elevated herself upon her hind paws and padded to the dais. Most maidens had seen her before, but as she kept largely to herself they did not know her. The maidens' eyes became wide at the sight of the paws, and when she faced them, and they gazed upon her tattoo and emerald encrusted forehead, their eyes became even wider. But what they were really reacting to was her power. "If I may, Morgan," she said, and then addressed the group.

First, she bowed. "My name is Dark Star MacLeod of Caithness. It is my privilege to have begun a very subtle communication with a being of the distant future. She is part faerie and her name is Axis. She exists far to the future, one thousand five hundred years hence. She was born to bring Avalon back from dormancy. But I also know that," and her purring voice dropped a few octaves, her glittering eyes surveying the inhabitants of the room, "I also know that her soul had an incarnation during the time Avalon was still alive and thriving. That could be now. The fact is that it is possible that one of you...one of us...is this Axis."

Dark Star let these words fall in a hush, and she stepped back. She sat on the dais next to Morgan, with her spotted paws sticking out from the folds of her skirts, and her front paws folded in her lap. A hint of the dragon wrist tattoos was visible to those of keen eye.

Morgan spoke. "The point is, my maidens, that if we could discover this soul counterpart of Axis, we would have a tangible connection through time; a thread, as it were, and we could run communication along that thread. We could help Axis bring Avalon back in the future, where it is very needed."

Dark Star rose and spoke again. "Maidens, this is what you must do. We all, every single one of us, will enter into a twenty four hour silent meditation. Be deep in your breathing. Access your inner resources more deeply than you ever have before. Dig new tunnels through your minds. Go beyond the depths of the caverns in your souls. And ask: *Is it me? And if not, then who is it?* We will not eat; we will only drink water from the Holy Well, and will rejoin here in this room, twenty four hours hence. Is this clear?"

It was so clear, in fact, that only a soft murmuring was heard as assent, with the gentle bobbing up and down of heads. With one paw extended towards the door, Dark Star purred, "You may go." And they filed out, silently.

As Morgan, Sage, and Dark Star walked along the path back to their dwelling, by torchlight they came upon a great blue heron, sitting in the middle of the path. This was strange, for it to have left the lake. It gave them the feeling that it had been waiting for them. It faced them, then turned and flew straight up, giving them the full view of its six foot wing span.

Ah, thought Dark Star, *it is a message from Axis, I am sure of it.*

"Order must come to the hall," spoke Morgan, up on the dais. "Let us all close our eyes together, and take three very deep breaths." At the conclusion of the breath taking, the maiden Wyrrd waded through the group of her sisters and approached the dais. Dark Star, seated next to Morgan, regarded her with a slightly raised brow, which caused a crinkle in her tattoo.

Wyrrd dropped into a combination bow-curtsey. "My elders of the Goddess," she spoke, in a grave and regal voice, "It is I. I who call myself Wyrrd. Axis and I share the same soul."

Out of the jaw-dropped silence, she continued. "It is imperative that we begin communicating with Axis straight away. She is starved of us, of Avalon, of magic. She hangs on by a thread, praying in her innermost heart that we will contact her."

By this point the other maidens had begun the jostling, the whispering. Some were jealous, some relieved. But as the whispering had begun, Morgan stood and spoke quickly. "All are dismissed. Resume your regular order of discipline." And she waved her hand to the door. The maidens began their exit, many craning their necks sideways and back, straining to see and hear any tidbit of information. The last flow of drapery moved through the door, and the sentry at that post closed it, and retreated.

They were alone: Morgan, Dark Star, Sage, and the maiden Wyrrd. Finally, Morgan inquired. "What does it feel like?"

"It feels like there is a thread finer than spider web which connects us, and I suppose that thread is the continuation of our soul...the thread stretches through layers of lifetimes...the soul is always the same, our characters are just different..."

"How did you know it was you?" asked Dark Star.

Wyrrd, who had long reddish locks, and green eyes, looked into the glitter of the eyes of Dark Star, and was tempted to say, "I just do." But knowing a more sacred translation was required of her, she consulted her innermost feelings before speaking. "Because during my meditation I slept, and a blue heron came into my dream. Lady Morgan has always taught us that the blue heron is the symbol of arcane knowledge. When I awoke from the dream, I knew then that it was not a dream, it was a visitation, and my instinct told me it was from Axis."

"Right, right, enough," uttered Dark Star gently, placing a forepaw upon the shoulder of Wyrrd. "Welcome, Lady, to this inner circle. You must work closely with us. You are now the primary link between Avalon and Axis—the future."

Wyrrd spoke: "My core instinct tells me that if we work together with a being of the future, like Axis, the magnetic pull between the future and the past—which is us, actually...the magnetic pull between our two time frames will generate a force field of power that will pull Avalon out of dormancy and back into reality!"

Dark Star gazed at the maiden Wyrrd as she uttered this last, and was pleased to see in Wyrrd's eyes the look of ascendance.

Three

THE INTERIOR WORLD OF
WYRRD

The maiden Wyrrd sat alone in her chamber. These were perhaps the moments she loved best. She surveyed the treasures of her long, velvet covered altar. There was her china dish full of semi-precious stones and spiral seashells (from her grandmother), and her vase of thick brown cattail reeds (from the Lake). There was holly, with red berries; and yellow, orange and red autumn leaves. There were feathers, some speckled, some striped, from owls, hawks, gulls and pheasants. Her favorite feather was from a blue jay—how the blue shimmered in the sun!

She had clusters of white cat whiskers sticking out of sea urchins; sand dollars and starfish; tufts of moss, pieces of lichen, pine cones and tree branches. There were deer antlers, tiny skulls (perhaps of rabbits); and a marine vertebra she had found at the cove near her family's house. She had a grey rock with a white zigzag streak, which reminded her of a lightning bolt. And a thick quartz crystal inside of which appeared to be a frozen landscape with a snow covered mountain.

Also upon the brown velvet were amethysts, turquoise, rhodochrosite and sujalite. There were butterfly wings, dead dragonflies, dried caterpillars, and ladybugs, and weaving through the whole array was the long skin of a snake. There was a giant petrified shark's tooth; and an egg-shaped grey rock with a perfect white ring. It looked rather like an eye, and Wyrrd was starting to suspect that the rock spirit looked out at her from within.

Her altar looked perhaps like a science laboratory, but it was arranged like a miniature landscape. She loved these things, and kept collecting them, and if asked why, she would say: "Because they soothe me." She was aware of the sacred nature of these items, and they connected her to God.

Wyrrd's room had one window. On fair days she was able to open it. At this time she called to her fox, which lived in the forest near her dwelling. "Shoonach! Come girl!" Within moments the small fox approached the window. She was the rusty-red color, not unlike Wyrrd's own hair. Shoonach (which means fox in Gaellic) had a white bib, white cheeks, white on the tip of her red tail, and black legs and feet. Wyrrd loved this little fox. She had found it as a tiny kit on one of her many walks in the wood and it appeared not to have a family. It was living in a hollow log. Wyrrd tended to love animals more than people, and took to bringing the tiny fox kit daily food, usually dried deer meat which she had softened in water from the sacred well. As Shoonach grew, she became more trusting and adventurous and began following Wyrrd back to her dwelling, oftentimes sitting outside her window.

Now it was fall. Shoonach's fur was thick and lush, and Wyrrd felt confident that Shoonach would be warm enough in winter, curled in a ball within her hollow log. *But if it ever becomes deathly cold—I will sneak her right into my chamber!* thought Wyrrd. Taking care of this animal was much more important to her than adhering to standardized rules of conduct.

Wyrrd climbed out of her window onto the ground, where fallen leaves created a thick carpet. There were many caterpillars now, the bushy brown and black type. Wyrrd stopped to watch them move. They rather flowed up and down towards their unknown destinations, like waves. Then she scooped Shoonach up into her arms. The fox was presently the size of a small cat.

"Let's go into the woods, girl," and after hugging Shoonach to her chest, Wyrrd let the fox back down to the ground where she trotted alongside. They walked, through the fallen leaves and fragrant air, toward one of Wyrrd's favorite places. It was not so much a place as much as it was a tree. It was a quite large, wide oak tree, heavily branched, and what Wyrrd especially loved about it was the leaves. In the fall, when most other tree's leaves were turning yellow, red, or orange, this particular tree's leaves turned a lovely shade of pink. It was the only tree Wyrrd had ever seen or heard of that turned pink. She and Shoonach arrived at the tree and immediately Wyrrd began observing the leaves.

The colour itself soothed her, because it emanated warmth. She stooped down and petted the little fox. Shoonach looked up at her, with bright, happy little eyes and an inquisitive snout, and for a moment Wyrrd felt tears well up in her at the sight of such innocent love. Shoonach loved her and she could truly feel it. "I will bring you into my chamber on cold, snowy winter nights—I swear it!" aloud she announced.

It is entertaining to watch young animals, for they forever sniff and pounce and prance, and for a while that is all Wyrrd did, is watch the fox. Then, she felt the Visitation. Shoonach issued a few sharp barks. At first it felt like wind. But not a normal wind, for it weaved in and out in a zigzag fashion, like a

145

lightning bolt. The pink leaves of the tree moved forward and back, and the long red locks about Wyrrd's face suddenly brushed her cheeks with force. The maiden Wyrrd saw a great raven descend to a tree branch, and then she heard words in her mind:

"Lady—I beseech you. I am so far away, it seems, and so detached from my past that it is almost like being blind and deaf. I need of you to prove you hear me, that you've gotten this message. You must send me signs, but because I am so deaf and blind, your signs must be blatant. I, Axis, await your response."

At this point, Shoonach was shuffling around at what looked to be a pile of leaves, and digging. She became quite excited. Wyrrd was reeling from her encounter, but was distracted by the actions of Shoonach and went to her. "Girl, what is it you've got?" And there, finally exposed, was a nest of bunnies. Baby rabbits, as it were. Tiny rabbit babies with brand new fur, golden brown. Wyrrd drew in breath sharply, and instantly looked at Shoonach. She picked Shoonach up. Because, endearing though she may have been, Shoonach was a fox, and this looked to be a plate of morsels of the highest degree to a fox. Shoonach strained to get out of Wyrrd's arms, pushing her forelegs against Wyrrd's chest.

"This will not do, Shoonach. It is imperative that these bunnies be saved. You will not eat, nor disturb them." But Wyrrd ached to have a better look at the rabbits, and could think of but one solution. As swiftly as ever, she carried her fox back through the forest to her dwelling. She pulled the window open from outside, and deposited Shoonach in the chamber. "Stay here, girl," Wyrrd said with a firm tone. And with one last look at the fox's pleading face, she pushed the window shut. And then she was off, crunching the dry leaves beneath her boots, walking more slowly and carefully as she came back to the pink oak tree.

Luckily the bunny nest remained undisturbed. But there was a new development. The mother rabbit had returned! She was lying on her side, and the tiny babies were nursing at her stomach. Wyrrd was filled with emotion. She was filled with the ecstasy of the love, sweetness, and gentleness she was observing in one of earth's most charming small animals.

Wyrrd knew this moment could not last long. She knew that any second, perhaps even this second, the mother would become aware of her, and scatter or bolt. Briefly her greatest desire flew through her mind. And that would be that she would approach the nest (with its leaf henge all around it) and be able to stare at, and even pet, the bunnies.

The mother rabbit still did not move. The babies continued to wriggle about, fur against fur, tiny paddle shaped paws walking over each other, tiny ears twitching, making small squeaking sounds, all attempting to get to the nipples of their mother. The mother too was brown, and she had a curious marking: centered right above her eyes, she had a white spot of fur.

Wyrrd, governed by a power much stronger than her mind, approached the nest. She knelt before it. One little rabbit took notice of her, and tears came to Wyrrd's eyes at the feeling in her heart when the little rabbit's eyes met her own. The rabbit, unperturbed, turned back to its purpose. Wyrrd remained kneeling. The mother rabbit opened her eyes. Because of her situation, she was able to observe Wyrrd. Nothing happened. Wyrrd smiled at the mother rabbit. She felt completely full, of all good things, love and peace and happiness. She reached out. She touched a baby. The fur was so soft she almost could not feel it. Her fingers were cold but the fur was warm. She saw the tiny white cotton tail. The baby rabbit did not object, so Wyrrd petted it. Then she petted another, and another. It was the most sweetness she had ever experienced in one sitting.

The great raven, which had been watching the entire encounter, flew away, as if on a sacred errand.

———————

Soft but insistent knocking upon her chamber door shook Wyrrd from her reverie.

At first she felt miffed. *I must reflect upon my visitation from Axis—and someone disturbs me!* she thought. But having been schooled in the wisdom of gentleness, Wyrrd drew a deep calming breath, collected herself and approached the door. She had no sooner opened it, and the maiden without burst into nervous dialogue: "Madame!" she coloured. "I mean, Lady...Wyrrd! Her—Highness—Dark Star wishes to speak to you!"

All at once Wyrrd realized that amongst her peers, she had risen in stature. This young woman barely knew how to address her! But Wyrrd, being calm by nature, soothed the girl. "I will always be Wyrrd, to you and all the other maidens. Nothing is different between us," and she stared straight into the pupils of the maiden's eyes, which is an enchantment, and the girl calmed.

"Now I must go!" Wyrrd grabbed a shawl from her bed, whisked it round her, and flew out the main entrance of the Hall of Maidens.

Dark Star sat alone in her tiny bedroom, which was within Morgan's dwelling. They had been using the branches of long dead apple trees for fire, which imparted to the woodsmoke a slightly sweet smell that Dark Star adored. Presently the smoke was wafting into her chamber, and it made for a perfect welcome for the arrival of the Maiden Wyrrd, who had just been announced.

When Wyrrd entered the room, there were three things she saw, while she gratefully breathed the sweet woodsmoke. First, she saw a vase of pussy willow branches, and the light from the window was touching them just so. The yellow light beams made the furry pods look like tiny mice, and Wyrrd wanted with all her might to touch them. Second, she became aware of a pouch of the finest velvet upon the bed. The pouch was twilight purple, darker than the deepest amethyst, and attached to it was a gold cross-shaped brooch inlaid with a giant white pearl. For a moment the violet shade of the pouch reminded Wyrrd of the evening sky on the edges of the faerie country.

Thirdly she saw Dark Star, who, though mighty in presence, had almost hidden herself until Wyrrd was ready to see her. Now, it seemed she took over the room. The emeralds upon her forehead glowed green. Beneath the star tattoo, her solemn brown eyes connected with Wyrrd's, and Wyrrd instantly sank into a deep curtsey, bowing her head.

The Purring Voice began: "Rise, enlightened one; you have no need to curtsey before *me*." And Wyrrd saw that she was smiling. "Is it true that you have already been contacted by Axis? Tell me all."

Wyrrd approached the pussy willow branches and began touching the fur of the pods. It was not unlike the rabbit fur. "You may take a branch," said Dark Star. Wyrrd's face lit up in joy, and she instinctively pulled out the branch which held the most pods. For Wyrrd, this was a substantial gift, and she beamed thanks at Dark Star, bowing her head.

"Sit down," Dark Star's paw gestured to a chair, and again she said, "Tell me all." Wyrrd stared into the soothing brown eyes and recounted the Visitation that occurred beneath the pink tree, how Axis beseeched her to send blatant signs, and for a reason she did not know, she also told Dark Star about the rabbit's nest. Dark Star said, "The zigzag wind, like a lightning bolt—that is Axis's symbol; it is her sign. For lightning and thunder are her Gods."

"You said, at the end of the assembly of discovery, that there is a thread finer than spider web that connects you; that the thread stretches through the layers of lifetimes....... Wyrrd. With...this...thread...you can reach through the layers of time." Here Dark Star paused. Then: "State again what she said about being deaf and blind."

"She said, 'I am so detached from my past that it is almost like being blind and deaf. You must send me signs, but they must be blatant.'"

Dark Star resumed her full height. She stood upon her spotted paws, and she held out her fore paws towards Wyrrd. "You must send her power. You must use the Thread. Send her dreams—of magic—of spirits— anything! You *are* her—you are Axis! This is

151

the way! This is the way we will bring Avalon back, so that it is real in the future—the future where Axis lives..." Dark Star was staring into space as she spoke, as if she could see whole worlds in front of her which to Wyrrd were invisible.

"We—must—conjure—magic," the purring voice continued. "Find out...who was close to her here...I know!...who are your closest friends? Because, Lady, your best friends were her best friends...and when souls are that close, they remain that way *always*..." Then, silence. Then, from the silence: "Foxleigh, Devon, Lawlor..." Wyrrd uttered the names of her closest companions.

"Well then. Call them to you. Speak. See if they can feel the future. And all of you join with me here on the morrow at first light. We travel to Dolbadarn Castle, otherwise known as Wildcat Tower."

With her pussy willow branch, Wyrrd walked back along the path to her dwelling, preparing her announcement.

The four maidens sat cross legged on Wyrrd's floor, upon which she was so fortunate as to have warm sheepskins, a gift of her father. "Sisters, you know what has befallen. You know of Axis," and then Wyrrd told them of her meeting with Dark Star, stressing the part about the Thread. Shoonach shuffled about on the sheepskins, curling up. Foxleigh, perhaps because of her name, felt closest to Shoonach, and petted her warm, red fur. Foxes can't purr but, if they could have, Shoonach would have, and she was doing a fine job pretending to. It was obvious the little fox liked the company.

Lawlor had red lips and she was quite pretty, while Devon had a most unusual feature: a large round freckle precisely in the center of her chin. Wyrrd continued. "From Axis's perspective, we are the past. And we have power, because Avalon is alive. But where Axis is in time, Avalon is not accessible within her reality. She needs our help, to bring Avalon back into existence in the future. We have the power and we must send it to her. These are Dark Star's orders, and they must be carried out."

Foxleigh, whose hair was so blond it was almost white, spoke. "What are we to do, Wyrrd?"

"You must all dream this night. The chance is strong that in the future, where Axis lives, you are all with her and close to her. But you must discover in what capacity. Dream this night with intent of discovery. Dark Star must not be kept waiting."

"So it's almost like reverse remembering - you want us to remember things that are happening in the future," said Lawlor.

Devon tilted her head to one side, in understanding. "Yes...it makes sense, about the thread...we must use this thread to connect our spirits of now to our spirits of the future...thereby reaching through the layers of time."

"Right! Exactly!" exclaimed Wyrrd, thankful for their understanding. "So: it is four days till Samhain. On the morrow we depart at first light." Foxleigh, Devon, and Lawlor's eyebrows shot up and their eyes opened wide. "These are the orders of Dark Star. We will travel with her to Dolbadarn Castle, which is also known as Wildcat Tower." Wyrrd could see upon their faces the excitement as this privilege set in. "But dream well and deeply, sisters, for Dark Star will want answers. You must know, by the morning time, who you are in the life of Axis." And with a smile full of wonder, Wyrrd bid them good night.

Four

WILDCAT TOWER

The horse's hooves clomped along slowly on the old roads, the sound muffled by mist. Shoonach trotted along with them. They were entering hilly country. Stags with large antlers darted in front of them, out of the moving mist. The mist came back and the stags were gone.

"We travel north and we travel west," purred Dark Star. "On the eve of our arrival, it will be Samhain. You all know well that this is the time of the year when the veils between the worlds are at their most thin." The maidens all stared at her. They were all in awe, and were very intent upon pleasing her. They were not scared; rather they already adored and revered her.

A light rain began to fall, and the priestesses were grateful for their heavy cloaks. Though it was autumn, the temperature was still agreeable. There had not yet been a frost. Dark Star held her reins in one paw. The maidens tried not to stare, but they could not steal enough glances at the spotted fur that poked out beneath Dark Star's black velvet. Finally, she laughed. It was a low purring sound, it sounded very warm, and it made the maidens feel comfortable. "Look as much as you like, daughters of the Goddess. My paws are a special gift from the depths of magic itself, and if they inspire endless staring, then I will humbly receive it."

When the maidens were not staring at the paws, they would sneak glances at the tattoos upon Dark Star's forehead and neck. Both were like ornaments and were charged with power like thunder. Finally, Devon gathered enough courage to speak. "Your Highness Dark Star," she began, and when that Lady looked upon her in a bright, welcoming manner, Devon relaxed and continued. "May I ask...the origin of your skin ornamentation?"

Dark Star smiled. Upon her countenance, which was so solemn and regal, a smile could have seemed out of place. But this time it was fitting. Her brown eyes lit up. "My tattoos were given to me as a child. It is the way of my ancestors."

"What of your crown of emeralds, Lady?" asked Lawlor. The maidens were relaxing, which was exactly Dark Star's desire. For the magic ahead, they needed to be as calm as possible. "The emerald is the totem stone of my clan, MacLeod. This headwear has been passed down in my family for centuries." And as Dark Star gazed upon Lawlor as she spoke, the pale rays of the sun struck the emeralds.

"If I may be permitted to say so, Lady, you look like an otherworldly queen, with the emeralds, the tattoos, and the spotted fur paws," said Foxleigh. It was the first thing she had ever said to Dark Star, and it felt good to her, to have spoken. Then Wyrrd: "While all of those things do indeed befit a queen, the truly sovereign aspect of Dark Star comes from within her—she has inner power." And that lady rode along and smiled mysteriously, keeping silent.

At the end of three days they arrived at a lake. The horses and Shoonach pushed through the cattail reeds to drink the water at its edge. Wyrrd marveled at the smallness of Shoonach's body, compared with those of the horses. She was compact, with her little hindquarters sticking out of the reeds, and her bright red tail with white tip. Shoonach was hard to look away from, because she was so easy to adore. Her sprightly antics, lush fur, and endearing face captivated her audience, which included all of the maidens and Dark Star. "You are a lovely animal," Dark Star purred softly, as she fed Shoonach a morsel of dried deer meat which the fox ate fervently. As Dark Star petted the fox, the animal looked up at her with innocence and curiosity. "I think there is nothing better than animals," Wyrrd uttered, as she reached down and picked Shoonach up, rubbing her cheek against her muzzle.

They all looked across the lake at the castle tower, which had the Snowdonia Mountains as a backdrop. The end of sunset was casting pure yellow light from the sky to the lake, and the water reflected it, suffusing the very air with gold. The castle tower was up on a hill, surrounded by twisting trees. "It is a holy time to have arrived," said Dark Star. "Now then, maidens, let us ascend the hill, where I think you will have a pleasant surprise."

She was right, as the entire hill was covered in moss. Moss as green as Dark Star's emeralds, coating the ground, thicker than grass. It coated the bases of the tree trunks, even. "This will have a different magic in the morning dew, for this moss sparkles like the sea," added Dark Star.

"But please, can we stay here for a little while?" questioned Foxleigh yearningly. She crouched down, feeling the moss with her open palms. Then she took off her boots, and stood, feeling the spongy soft coolness radiate up through her limbs. Eventually they all followed suit, while Shoonach sniffed about the gnarly trees.

After a light meal of dried fruit and barley bread, and water from the sacred well (which they had brought with them), the group sat down around a fire in the great hall. Wildcat Tower, or Dolbadarn Castle, was primarily one large round stone structure, with a few small open windows. It was named so due to the proliferation of wild cats living in the vicinity. It had recently been vacated, which Dark Star knew, but the reason she chose it for a ceremony was its situation. On one side were the Snowdonia Mountains, home to the ancient magicians the Pheryllt; on another side, the lake. It was high up on a hill, surrounded by the tall gnarled trees. This was also an area known to produce a lot of thunder and lightning, and Dark Star knew that those gods were needed, to send every bit of power possible through the layers of time to Axis.

Shoonach was curled close to the fire, but not too close—Wyrrd made sure her fur was safe from being singed. Ancient gold and silver banners of the castle's clan still hung on the walls—no doubt because they would be returning—and the banners emanated the vibrations of the clan, bearing images of lynxes. The women sat upon their cloaks in a circle: Dark Star, Wyrrd, Lawlor, Foxleigh, and Devon. "You know why we are all here," uttered Dark Star. "Let us engage in a commencement meditation. Close your eyes, all of you."

There is something that happens when one sense is cut off—other senses are heightened. After only a few deep breaths the maidens became aware of the thickness of the silence: it was glistening, pulsating, and sounded almost frosted. Waves of wind washed over the tower. Quite suddenly, a lightning bolt flashed, sending sharp beams of light into the tower through the high, small windows. Dark Star began purr-chanting, and they did not know at first if her words were an incantation or a dream: "Last night I dreamt of a dragon. It was tall and walking through the forest with large teeth. It was a message from Axis."

"You see, she wants us to send her blatant signs, but she is sending us blatant signs as well. It is now the time for each of you maidens," she gestured with her paw towards Wyrrd's companions, "to reveal who you are in the future—in the life of Axis. Who would like to begin?" And her eyes followed them as they looked from one to the other.

The power of the fire and the lightning enveloped Foxleigh and ignited her. "I would, Lady. I dreamed that I was an old woman, with grey hair. I wore my hair piled upon my head in a bun. I wore opal earrings. I used to give tea to a little girl. It was my great granddaughter. It was Axis. I was her great grandmother."

"Foxleigh," Wyrrd whispered, interrupting, "I beg you pardon my interruption, but I do not understand. If we are speaking of the future, why then do you speak in the past tense?"

"Because I am dead," said Foxleigh in a slow voice. "I died a long time ago, when Axis was very young. But I tell you—I was her great grandmother…" and her voice trailed off, in remembrance.

Dark Star knew the hallowed sound of the truth, and had a satisfied look upon her countenance. She nodded approval to Foxleigh; then she raised her eyebrows at Lawlor. "I was Axis's grandmother," said Lawlor, smiling, her red lips shining. "We were very close, and I brought her everywhere with me. She was my favorite grandchild, and my only granddaughter."

Wyrrd broke in—"Again—you use past tense—is it that you too have died?"

"Yes. I died very recently, only two years ago. But I go to Axis in her dreams, and I visit her, and remind her that I am still alive—that my spirit is still alive!" The fire cracked loudly.

"How is it that fire always knows what we are saying?" Dark Star mused, smiling. "And now—Devon?"

Devon used the sight of Dark Star's paws, which were resting in her lap, and the sound of her purring cat voice, to gather strength for her delivery. "Lady—sisters—I know this may sound strange, but..." She met the eyes of them all: Wyrrd's green eyes, calm yet intense, Foxleigh's pale blue soft eyes, inquiring, Lawlor's loving eyes that seemed to encompass all colors, and finally, Dark Star's dark brown eyes, trusting and soothing. Where Devon thought she would not be believed, she could tell instantly that she had been wrong. Dark Star believed her before she even spoke. *And why would she not?* thought Devon. *She is part cat.*

Devon breathed in deeply and delivered her announcement: "I was the family cat of Axis for twenty three years. I was most close to Axis and her mother. I died nine years ago, but always I have gone to Axis in dreams and showed her that I was still alive."

"I had grey and white fur, and—my white chin had in its center a perfect circle of grey fur." She stared at them all, and they all stared at her chin. Her chin, with its large, perfectly circular freckle in the center. Just then a lightning bolt blazed through the windows. Thunder cracked, and then it rumbled, and it sounded like a language.

"Axis is communicating with us. I told you," and Dark Star looked directly at Wyrrd, "I told you lightning and thunder are her gods." Their fire had now burned low. The red-orange coals were making that crinkling sound, like thin ice cracking. Dark Star bestowed her countenance upon Foxleigh, Devon and Lawlor. "I acknowledge you all for your excellent divining. Truth has its very own vibration...your conjuring has impressed me...obviously, you are all very clear..." her eyes took on a faraway glaze, as if she were focusing upon that which is intangible. The three maidens felt honored and proud. It felt good to be believed, especially by Dark Star.

"We will now prepare to send Axis a message," announced Dark Star. "Wyrrd, if you please, place your nature totems."

Wyrrd had brought with her many special things from the collection in her chamber, and now set about arranging them in a circle, near the fire. There was holly, with red berries; her pussy willow branch; pine cones, and cattails. There were pink leaves from her favorite tree, hawk feathers, moss tufts, and lichen. And a brown and black caterpillar. She put the caterpillar in the center, along with a quartz crystal. "Dark Star, I feel it is important that you place your purple pouch in the center, as well. Definitely with that pearl on it."

Dark Star did as such, and the maidens all marveled at the way she deftly used her paws to place the pouch perfectly, not disturbing anything else. The orange glow of the dying fire made the purple shade of Dark Star's velvet pouch even more rich. The pearl, inlaid in the gold cross-shaped brooch, was a domed shimmering mirror. "Wyrrd," said Foxleigh, very quietly, "Why do you have a caterpillar here?"

"The caterpillar is the butterfly before it can fly. And I am sure Axis loves caterpillars, because I do...and...I *am* Axis—you see?"

"Someone—stoke the fire," ordered Dark Star, and Lawlor jumped at the chance. Within minutes the new kindling crackled into flames, catching onto the larger logs Lawlor had stacked, and now the tower was again full of light.

"See the fur...upon the caterpillar, the pussy willow pods," purred Dark Star's cat voice. "These fur covered nature beings are symbols of softness, warmth, and gentleness. These subtle characteristics are needed to send power." Only Dark Star noticed that a raven had come to perch upon one of the high window ledges. She then produced a sharp silver needle. "Maidens one and all, we've spoken of the thread. To connect your spirits of now to your spirits of the future, thereby sending power to Axis, you must use your blood. Blood is part of the thread. Blood trickles down through lifetimes, through bodies...blood is magic, because it carries life, but it also keeps the soul connected across lifetimes—hence the term—bloodline..."

Pricking their fingers one by one, they all squeezed their blood droplets into the center of the circle where the crystal, the caterpillar, and the purple pouch were. "Good," said Dark Star, and she nodded her approval. "Now see this," and she pointed her paw to the stones of the inner wall of the tower. At first the maidens saw nothing but shadows flickering over the stone, but with greater intent, they saw that towards which Dark Star gestured. It was a single strand of spider silk, extending upwards, as far as they could see. It seemed to have no end.

As soon as Dark Star knew they could all see the strand, she began to chant, and the maidens knew to close their eyes. At first it sounded like purring, but then they could hear words: "We call upon the Great Raven, the Carrier of Ceremonial Messages, to fly through the layers of time and deliver this message unto Axis, who is the future incarnation of The Maiden Wyrrd:

"A thread connects us, fine as spider web. This thread exists only Now, in the pristine gem of the Present. For us to feel it—to travel feeling across it like a tightrope—we must be alive, awake, conscious and walking the vista of this eternal moment. We connect with you in this one instant among trillions. Now there is no distance. Now there is no space. Your country lies on the inside of our eyelids: We stalk you. We touch you, within the Holy Now.

"We inject power into your soul. We send you the power of Remembrance. Remember your Self at Avalon. We send you blatant visions, by blood, fire, and spider web." The raven upon the window ledge squawked loudly three times, and flew off.

Then the loudest thunder crack any of them had ever heard came in answer. That is when the maidens knew for certain that thunder is a language.

When many minutes later they had finally opened their eyes, a most miraculous thing had transpired. The caterpillar that had been in the center of Wyrrd's circle was gone.

———————

Far away, on a tiny island on a different continent, the Lady Axis received a message. It came through time and through space, and it came in the form of a dream. She dreamed that five ghosts came to her on horseback. Five female grey ghosts, all riding live horses, in a straight line across, riding straight towards her.

Five

WITHIN THE GATEWAY TREE

All the while they had been gone, Sage had been meditating, keeping silent. She did not even speak to the Lynx. It was coming to her what needed to happen next. And she began to think about the Gateway Tree. Sage was in her chamber that was part of Morgan's dwelling. The Lynx was curled upon her bed, purring, and she stroked his thick fur as she pondered. The cat seemed to almost be smiling. Sage marveled at the long tufts at the tips of his ears, there to catch sound.

Finally, she broke her silence. "Come, boy," she said to him, and they ventured out of doors. She led the way down along the Lake, where red berries abounded and the cattails had blown out, now all shaggy and

167

furry. She loved the autumn. Her birthday, November first, had just passed the day before. Morgan had given her an ancient brass key. "Keep this as a reminder that the keys to opening gateways are often calmness and gentleness," she had said. Sage had placed the key upon her personal altar.

Her destination was a cavernous hollow tree near the Tor. She looked up at the seven stones, the seven upright megaliths in a circle atop the Tor. The tall stones emanated their eerie power. Sage felt a soothing feeling from being near them. She was glad the Gateway Tree was so close to those stones. The Gateway Tree had lost most of its leaves. They had been a warm, golden yellow, glowing like unpolished gold in the dim sunlight. By now the ground was strewn with them, and there were only a few still attached to the branches. These waved lightly in the soft wind. The tree's bark was coated in ancient lichen.

It was so quiet. Sage and the Lynx approached the tree. If she crouched down, she could just squeeze in through the hole at its base. It was much easier for the Lynx, who just strolled right through. Within it was fairly dark. There was another hole, much smaller, far above Sage's head, and light beamed in through it. The diameter of this tree was perhaps four feet.

Sage sat cross legged on the thick mossy ground, her back up against the inside of the trunk. The Lynx stretched out in front of her.

Together they took up almost all the space. The Lynx began purring. Sage could tell he liked it in there. Cats like dark corners. She leaned against the strong trunk wall and breathed. The air was pungent with the earth smell, and moist from the moss. The old smell of autumn crept into her nostrils. *If wisdom could have a smell, this is it,* she thought. And with this contemplation she fell into a sleeplike trance, and eventually she heard a voice inside of her head that was coming from far away.

There was only one other time that the Goddess spoke inside of Sage's mind. It was when she was inside of the Tor. This time, the voice said: "The Lady Axis's destiny is to Remember. She does not have a teacher. It is her destiny to remember her self from the past, from Avalon, and thereby teach her self all she remembers. This makes her the shaman *and* the apprentice. It is an experiment—a spirit test. If she succeeds she will have invented her own magic.

"As you know, within standard earth reality, Avalon will be attacked soon. The people who attempt to destroy Avalon also destroy all records of its existence, because they do not want anyone to remember it or know that it ever existed. This is because Avalon is of the power of woman, and the destroyers only believe in the power of man, and they believe there is only one god, and they believe that god is actually a male spirit.

"As the centuries go by, after Avalon's displacement, it is more and more believed to be only the stuff of legend. By the time of Axis's life, most people have not even heard of it, and of those that have, almost all believe it was simply a made up story to tell around campfires. Axis's destiny is this: to bring about worldwide remembrance. You, Sage, began this work, by tapping in to the comprehensive global memory and igniting it. However, much more remembrance needs to occur. How does Axis remind people that Avalon was real, when they always want proof? This is where we come in. The more memory and omens and signs and symbols we can send her, the better. That is what she will have to work with. The fact is, the truth never dies."

The last sentence kept reverberating in her head. *The truth never dies. The truth never dies. The fact is, the truth never dies.* And Sage came out of the trance.

When she arrived on the doorstep of Morgan's house, she still had the glassy, dreamy expression of one who has seen god. Morgan knew she was coming, and opened the door. The moment Morgan saw Sage's eyes her mouth fell open. Sage's pupils were so dilated that Morgan thought she could see all of space within them. They were so deep, she could see into Sage's soul. Morgan embraced her gently. In her otherworldly language, she whispered, "Come sit by the fire, sister. Do not speak until you are ready." Sage allowed herself to be led to the low bench in front of the fire, and the Lynx took up his place as guardian. He sat straight up next to her feet, and it was very clear: until Sage resumed her normal countenance, he was in charge.

If not for the utter solemnity of the moment, Morgan would have found the Lynx's seriousness comical. But not in this instance. She went to make tea, while Sage stared glassy eyed into the orange flames. Everything made sense. She put out one hand and placed it on the Lynx's back, but did not pet him. She could not think, nor did she want to. The mechanisms that move in the human brain that create thoughts had reached a point of stillness.

"Morgan," she finally said, very slowly, as if it was the first time in her life she had ever spoken. "The Goddess has spoken to me, from within the Gateway Tree. I carry important messages about Axis and Avalon, but they are long and sacred and I may only say them once. When does the party return?"

Morgan placed a hot cup into Sage's cold hands, and sat next to her. They both stared at the crackling fire flames. "I expect their return two days hence. Can it wait that long?"

"It will have to." But looking at Morgan, she did not know how she could wait so long.

Six

THE WEB SPREAD

She was sure that if she touched it, her finger would get wet. Sage was holding in her left hand the very first card she had ever investigated—the one with the lake and trees, which had had a beaver swimming around so long ago. This time there were no beavers—yet—but Sage was staring deeply at the waters of the lake. They were moving, as were the treetops in the wind. She became mesmerized. She had to find out. Was it really wet? Softly, with the tip of her index finger, Sage touched the water. It broke the seal. The tip of her finger was touching real water. She pulled it back, and instantly circular ripples radiated away from the spot, causing tiny waves in the lake, which finally sloshed the shores.

Sage looked at the tip of her finger. It held one droplet of beautiful, magical water, and instinctively she rubbed it into her forehead, right between the eyes. If she thought that perhaps this was the extent of the card's gift to her on this morn, the kingdoms of magic had one more offering. Just as she was about to slide the card back into the deck, she saw something moving on the left side of the lake, right near a beaver lodge. A mother beaver moved out into the center of the lake, quite on the surface of the water, her big flat paddle tail quite in view. Upon it, nestled next to each other, were four baby beavers. They were going for a ride upon their mother's tail. Four tiny paddle tails, four miniature faces with the gnawing teeth showing—looking around at their new world. She watched until the mother beaver swam out of sight.

Sage finally replaced the card in the deck. Before today she had not known that the cards had a delicate surface tension, that once broken, could give access to the interior. At this time she was within the center of the ring stones, on top of the Tor. It was early morning, and the arc of the new moon was still visible in the sky. It hung on the horizontal, like a smile. Sage had come to the Tor specifically to conduct a major card spread. It was the morning after her experience within the Gateway Tree, and she still had this one more day before Dark Star and the maidens returned from Wildcat Tower.

Her inner core had instructed her to do the spread. She laid out a purple and green Indian tapestry on the ground before her. Then she meditated. She felt full of goodness, and relaxation became her. Sage did not know that much about Axis but she felt connected to her—surely they shared a common cause; and it was as if Axis were reaching her hand through time and space and beckoning to her. To the cards she chanted internally, *Tell me about Axis*, over and over. The wind spoke amongst the stones. As Sage meditated she could feel Axis. Axis's energy felt catlike but very soft, like a rabbit. With these feelings of Axis running through her fingers, Sage shuffled the thick cards and laid them out, facedown, in the shape of a spider web: one in the center with a full circle around it.

When she opened her eyes, her circle was before her, and all she could see as yet were nine purple backs with lightning bolts, with a paw print stamped across each one. Sage began turning the cards over. The card spread was so auspicious that it had the appearance of being contrived, as if Sage had purposely chosen an array of powerful cards. Goosebumps rose on her arms.

At the top of the circle in the north position, the place of wisdom, there lay the wisewoman card. Within the card was a shaman woman, and she wore a crown upon her head. The crown was of white spiral seashells, and sticking straight out from the center of these shells was a mass of jagged, elongated red coral branches. It looked like she wore a rack of deer antlers while lightning bolts were entering her brain. The crown seemed to elevate the woman, and she stood with her bare feet barely touching the mossy earth. She had light blond hair, and green eyes, and a slightly otherworldly, expressionless face. Sage knew it was Axis.

But she disciplined herself, putting the card back in place upon the tapestry. She disciplined herself to read the story of the web of cards. A card spread like this was to be read center first; then traveling up to the northwest position, then around sunwise, and back to the west. The early morning sun warmed Sage's hair as she began her task. She spoke softly to herself as she read the story of the cards. "So Axis's essence is true love!" For the center card was the love card, showing a man and a woman joined in matrimony, with a castle high up on a hill behind them. The love in their eyes was pure and ancient. "And in the northwest, she follows her instinct and intuition...then Axis herself as wisewoman in the north...then the sea, which means she is willing to take a risk...for her destiny...and the path...leads to Avalon!" Sage picked this card up, the one in the south position. It was the card that represented magic, and she was looking in on Avalon itself, with its apple trees, shimmering lake, wattle and daub dwellings, and the Tor with its seven standing stones. A shiver went down her spine as she squinted at the Tor within the card, and she saw herself, so tiny, in the center of the stones.

She put the card down abruptly, looked away from the spread, and took a deep breath. *How is it possible?* she thought. Suddenly she heard Artos's voice inside of her mind: *Magic has no rhyme or reason. Do not try to understand it, because you can not. Magic is part of the unknowable.* Again she breathed, staring at the stones around her, for strength.

There were only two cards left. "The bed...that means she is safe... and the castle in the west means...her dreams will manifest..." Sage stared at the castle, her memory flickering briefly upon the time when she had gone there, assisted by the orange wildcat. *This is quite a spread. It says clearly that Axis has a heart of true love; that she is a wisewoman, and her destiny is Avalon, and that she is assured success—because Artos told me the castle represents regality, success, and manifestation of dreams...*

Suddenly Sage remembered the Goddess's speech from within the Gateway Tree, for she had memorized it: *Axis's destiny is this: to bring about worldwide remembrance...you, Sage, began this work...how does Axis remind people that Avalon was real, when they always want proof? The more memory and omens and signs and symbols we can send her, the better...the fact is, the truth never dies.*

Her reverie was jolted by the sudden presence of Dark Star. First, from her sitting position, Sage saw only spotted leopard paws weaving through the grass between folds of black velvet. She elevated her eyes. The Lady Dark Star extended her forepaws in greeting. "I returned early to assist you. I saw in my great pearl what you were about. This is very auspicious, Sage ..." Dark Star gazed upon the glittering, glowing, moving card spread. With both paws she picked up the wisewoman card, staring at Axis. "Ah, she is a Norwegian beauty," she purred under her breath. She looked back at Sage and she again purred. "You know what you must do: you must go *in here*. You must visit Axis, and discover all you can from her." These were orders, but coming from Dark Star, they sounded to Sage like the most sacred of enchantments.

"Yes, Lady, I was just coming to that conclusion myself, upon your arrival." Giving the card back to Sage, Dark Star smiled. "I wait patiently for you within Morgan's chambers." And she inclined her head, turned swiftly in flows of velvet, and descended down the edge of the Tor.

Even though Dark Star had surprised her, Sage could only feel blessed and elevated by her visitation. It gave her confidence; there was something about Dark Star that made Sage feel high and triumphant. With these feelings, she did as Artos had taught her. First she meditated, to tap into the magic vein, where lives the very matrix of magic. Then she uttered the incantation, in a low voice: "Parasamgate."

As if on cue the Lynx arrived, to stand sentinel. Sage's body slumped to the ground, and with his strong muzzle, the Lynx nudged her into a more comfortable position. Then he sat right up against her to keep her body warm.

Seven

AXIS AND SAGE

Sage opened her eyes. She was in the middle of a tremendous lake, upon a tiny piece of earth that was so small it could not even be called an island. If it was an island, it was the smallest one in existence. It was round, furred with soft bright green grass, and was only large enough to accommodate the presence of perhaps two people. If Sage had laid down and extended her arms, her fingertips would touch water on one side while her toes would touch water on the other.

There was nothing upon the miniature island except herself, at first. She didn't know where she was, and she didn't care. She knew she was within the wisewoman card, to see Axis, and that is all she needed to know.

There was not one molecule of fear within her. Feeling this deep peace, she closed her eyes again, and breathed in the smell of pine being carried on the breeze from the shores. The edges of the lake were rimmed with giant conifers which had sweeping green boughs and immense pine cones.

Feeling a presence, Sage opened her eyes. And there, standing right in front of her, was Axis.

Axis smiled serenely. She looked happy to see Sage. But she did not speak. She tilted her head sideways, and continued to smile. It was a smile of deep satisfaction, and lightness, and Sage thought how Axis reminded her of Dark Star. Axis had long straight blond hair and green eyes, green like Dark Star's emeralds. She was still wearing her seashell and coral headdress. It looked like she was wearing a crown of orange lightning.

"So, Lady, we have come full circle. Finally we meet face to face." This was the first thing Axis said. Sage did not know what she meant, but felt confident that she would find out.

Sage stared into Axis's green eyes. "Finally?"

"Yes, you see, you have been coming to me, so strongly and purely, that I have written many pages of you..."

Sage knew not how to respond as she was somewhat shocked, so she simply stood and

tted out from the walls to form tiny
here were two wooden stools near
and a round wooden table. There
two windows; one looked out onto
the other into the depths of forest. It
quiet Sage could hear bird wings
eating the air. Upon Axis's table lay
writing tablet, with strange
s. Sage stared at the foreign writing.
d vaguely familiar. Nestled at the
was a long thin cylindrical item,
at one tip. It was quite obvious that
a writing instrument, but Sage had
en anything like it.

heard Dark Star's words in her
e must project ourselves, our power
gic and force, into the future where
a connecting point waiting, wanting to
us. She is mostly a human being; her
Axis.
s? Is this writing from the future?"
m your perspective it is, Sage. But
write for me? Anything—it would be
aningful for me." Axis held out the
instrument to Sage. Again Sage heard
tar's purring voice, *She needs our help*
h as we need hers. And the Goddess's
The Lady Axis's destiny is to
ber. The more memory and omens and
and symbols we can send her, the

e spoke softly: "To help
emember?"

stared and Axis continued. Axis had a strong
voice; she spoke a different form of English,
and had an unusual accent. "Now we are on
the same page."

Sage knew not what to make of this talk,
and finally spoke. "Axis—I know not of what
you speak, but I am here on orders—orders
from Dark Star. I am to...discover all I can
from you."

Axis's eyebrows raised high. "Rather, it is
I who would like to be discovering from
you...the truth must be made as tangible as
possible, or else my people will not believe..."
her voice trailed off, blending with the wind.
A crow cawed loudly overhead.

"Did you send me the blue heron at
night?" Axis asked.

Sage's vision blurred temporarily, and
now she almost lost her balance. Axis
reached out to steady her. Sage was
remembering the night of the assembly of
discovery, when she, Morgan, and Dark Star
had come upon the blue heron in the dark.
Dark Star had told them later: *It was a*
message from Axis—I am sure of it.

Sage, who also had green eyes, looked
deeply into Axis's pupils. In a shocked
whisper, she uttered: "Rather, Lady, we
thought it was you who sent the blue heron
to us......"

As they stared at each other in awe, and
thinking how alike they looked, a slithering
sound broke the silence, and it came from

between their feet. They looked down to see a snake curving its way through the grass. It crossed the tiny island, and then, just as the women thought it would enter the water, it curled into a spiral at the water's edge, and stared up at them.

"What do you think he's saying," whispered Sage, unable to unlock her eyes from the snake's gaze.

"First, he may be a she. Second, instinct tells me that we are but servants of the Great Spirit, and that we may never understand some things. All we can do is try to uncover buried truths."

The snake seemed so satisfied with this delivery that she uncoiled, and slithered straight into the water.

Hearing the word "instinct" sparked Sage's memory, and she now thought of the card spread. "So you do use your instinct..." Seeing the entire spread in her mind, with the castle in the west position, she blurted: "You will have success in manifestation of your destiny...that is what the cards said; and you know that the cards never lie."

Axis's smile was now even bolder than before, but she kept her lips closed, and stared off into space with her head tilted sideways. The smile faded into a peaceful blank stare. After some moments she looked back at Sage. "You drew cards of me?"

"Indeed, Lady, a whole great spread. I wish you could see my cards! In fact—that is

how I came to b
world of the w
am!"

Axis smiled
clear to Sage tha
Sage spoke. "C
home." Axis ges
hand towards o
looked closely, s
dwelling. Wisps o
from a single chim

The house lool
not imagine how
there was quite a l
and that shore. "V
like wands upon th
at the distance acro
there is a band
green...extending....
look and intend to w

Sage obeyed, and
became thicker and
rather like blurry str
colour. They walked
way, and the intent l
bare feet. At the op
only dissolved right
which point Sage's
followed Axis to the
small, it looked like o
it, but once inside, it s

Axis deftly stoked h
of the dwelling was

stones ju
shelves.
the fire,
were only
the lake,
was so
outside,
an ope
characte
It seeme
binding
pointed
this was
never se

Sage
mind: V
and m
there is
receive
name is

"Axi

"Fr
will yo
very m
writing
Dark S
as mu
words:
Remen
signs
better.

Sa
you...

Axis's face lit up, as if the very word 'remember' were an elixir. Sage sat on a stool, picked up the writing device, and set about writing. Axis watched, mesmerized. Her favorite character was the *edh*, which looked like this: ð. Sage was happy to be providing Axis with such joy over something so simple. But it was not considered simple by Axis. When she had done, Sage looked about the single room again. It occurred to her that there was not a substantial bed area, only a wooden cot in the corner, with brightly colored cushions adorning it.

"Axis, do you live here all of the time?"

Axis stood by the window which looked out across the lake. She turned from the view and looked at Sage. "The spirit of a soul has many facets, and these multiple facets live side by side simultaneously, like the face of a *diamond*," she delivered, placing emphasis on the final word. "Thus, we may occupy multiple lives at the same time. I have come here, to this lake, to meet with you, but I also exist on other planes.

"From the perspective of Now being a totality of all times, the spirit of my soul is living in all of my incarnations; for example, my spirit and Wyrrd's spirit are the same. Wyrrd and I send each other messages through time—through fifteen hundred years. She lives in the memory of my soul. To answer your question, a part of me lives here part of the time. But the part of me that you and Dark Star and the other priestesses are trying to contact lives somewhere else, somewhere very dense. It is there that the people do not readily believe in magic; it is there that they require solid proof for anything to be believed. These people are in great suffering, and it is my destiny to attempt to bring them Avalon—to bring Avalon back, into *that* world, so that magic may touch them."

"And this place is in the future, forward fifteen hundred years?"

"From your perspective, that is correct. I must take you back, now, Sage," said Axis, and Sage looked saddened. She wanted to ask more questions, but she knew to defer to Axis's authority.

"Do not be sad, we will be together again, I swear it," and Axis put her hand on her heart.

She guided Sage back across the lake, across the purple and green bands, to the grassy little island for her departure.

Eight

THE PRESENCE OF MERLIN

When Sage came back into her body upon the Avalon Tor, the seven stones still surrounded her, and the Lynx still stood sentinel. Dark Star was there, looking solemn. The Lynx licked Sage's face, which further revived her. *The smells are different here,* she thought groggily, as early morning mist entered her nostrils, carrying the scent of decaying leaves. The smell was high and wise.

"You must rest deeply, until tomorrow when the maidens return," purred Dark Star authoritatively. But it was welcome news. "Then you may tell us everything." And to Morgan's warm chambers Sage was led, where she slept peacefully, enveloped in her cocoon of magic.

Once Sage had revived, she related the Goddess's message from the Gateway Tree to Morgan, Dark Star, Wyrrd, Devon, Lawlor and Foxleigh. In turn they shared with her what had occurred at Wildcat Tower. They told her of the thunder and lightning speaking to them directly, and of the missing caterpillar at the end of the ceremony.

"Dark Star, how could that happen?" murmured Foxleigh.

Dark Star regarded them all with an austere gaze. "I would think that Axis's spirit entered the tower within a lightning bolt, and removed the caterpillar while all of our eyes were still closed."

"But how can that happen, literally? How can a physical thing be brought between the worlds—through time and through space?" asked Sage urgently.

"There are aspects of the kingdoms of magic that are unknowable. That is why they are magic. Do not try to understand the unknowable; in doing so you rob yourself of wonder. Being in awe is a sacred place in which to dwell," Dark Star purred. "Would you have it that the goddess reveals all of her secrets? Sage, what did you discover from Axis?"

Sage did not have to reflect. The most prominent thing regarding Axis that must be shared with all was this: "When I told her I had orders to discover all I could from her, she said rather it was she who would like to be discovering from me...she said, 'The truth must be made as tangible as possible, or else my people will not believe.' And she asked me if we sent her the blue heron at night!"

Most of the maidens knew not what to make of such an announcement, but Dark Star and Morgan looked at each other knowingly. Wyrrd and her friends kept their mouths closed. A hush had fallen over the room, and betwixt cracklings from the fire, all that could be heard was the sound of breathing.

Finally, Dark Star spoke: "It is clear what she means. Sage. Please repeat what the Goddess said to you within the Gateway Tree—the part about people wanting proof."

Since she had memorized the monologue of the goddess, Sage began readily: " 'How does Axis remind people that Avalon was real, when they always want proof? And this is where we come in. The more memory and omens and signs and symbols we can send her, the better. That is what she will have to work with. The fact is, the truth never dies.' "

Dark Star nodded. Now she turned towards Wyrrd. "You remember she wanted blatant visions. Well now it seems she wants something completely tangible, something physical...the same way she took your caterpillar, she needs us to send her something, from Avalon. And deliver it to her realm, right where she lives."

Morgan, who had so far been silent during the meeting, gave authoritative directions. "Nothingness has many wondrous caverns, within which to meditate. We all must become utterly blank in our minds, to receive instruction from the very forces where miracles are made. Go to the deepest recesses of your consciousness, and then go beyond even that. Enter the void, and live there. After the passing of some days I do believe we will know how to proceed."

Dark Star seconded these directions with a nod. In silence, she gestured with her paws for the maidens to depart the chamber. All filed out, leaving Sage with Morgan and Dark Star. "Someone is going to have to go between the worlds," Dark Star uttered. "Someone who Axis is very close to–with whom she has a deep connection." She stared around the room, resting her gaze finally upon a staff of blackthorn leaning against the wall in a corner, quite in the shadows. It emanated an eerie greenish glow.

"That's Merlin's staff, it is not, Morgan?"

"Yes. He left it behind last time he visited, saying he would return for it soon."

"Summon him here, if you would, please! As soon as possible."

Sage's mouth gaped at the way Dark Star delivered her order, even more so because of whom it involved. *Merlin! Dark Star had the*

authority to demand the presence of Merlin?
What Sage did not know, was that Dark Star and Merlin were dear old friends and colleagues, of many lifetimes.

"Certainly, Lady," replied Morgan calmly. And Sage proceeded to become excited at the prospect of beholding Merlin again. The last time she had seen him had been within the Tor, with Jesus the Christ.

When Dark Star and Sage had quitted the chamber, Morgan rose to take up the blackthorn staff of Merlin, and returned to sit in front of her fire. She held it reverently across her lap, tracing her fingers over the carved symbols. Moons, lightning bolts, stars—they were recognizable to anyone. But the vast array of esoteric symbols, they would be only known to an initiate of the mysteries. Morgan knew all of these runic characters and ogham glyphs. Touching them made the magic enter her body, and she shivered with knowing.

She held the staff up. The flames from the fireplace threw uneven orange light upon the staff, and Morgan summoned the House of the Raven Spirit, to deliver her message. "I pray to the Great Raven, courier of sacred messages! Make it be known to the Great Merlin, High Magician, that Avalon needs him, now."

Morgan knew that it did not matter where Merlin was, how far away in time, or space. He would arrive readily, she knew that. She went to sleep in her bed, expecting his imminent arrival.

Sage, who had been lying in a deep, peaceful sleep, was awakened in a most unusual manner. The Lynx was upon her, pressing her torso with his giant paws, and making insistent purring sounds. *He is not usually so excited, first thing in the morning,* was her groggy thought.

It was not morning; it was quite the middle of the night, and the first person to be aware of Merlin's arrival was the Lynx. He had heard and smelled him—knew him—and simply wanted Sage to unlatch the chamber door. He had heard someone enter the dwelling, and pricked up his tufted ears; he then heard the fire coals being reactivated, and a blaze stoked. By this time the Lynx's attuned nostrils had picked up Merlin's scent, and he remembered: the man from the caves of the Tor.

Now the Lynx was scratching on the door, which lead out to the common room. Sage too heard sounds by now, and at first wondered why Morgan, or Dark Star, was either up so late or so early. The Lynx looked at her, and in the dim light of her chamber, she saw the light in his eyes, and she knew by his look, that something was afoot. Then she remembered last eve's final words, of the summoning of Merlin, and she knew: *he is here!*

With haste and dexterity she dressed in the dark, donning appropriate garb, even fastening her amethyst amulet from Morgan around her neck. She hoped she looked fitting for the occasion. More so to silence the Lynx than because she was ready, she finally unlatched the door of the chamber.

Merlin's back was to her, as he faced the flames. The Lynx practically bounded to him like a dog, and Sage came near to laughing. Immediately upon reaching him the Lynx began purring vigorously. As if to give Sage a few more moments of privacy, Merlin paid attention only to the Lynx, and did not yet turn round. He spoke in the otherworldly language, like that of Morgan, thick like water in a stream. Sage readily deciphered it:

"Ah, it is you! The beautiful cat!" and he commenced petting, stroking, and patting the Lynx, who continued to be boisterous. "You are happy to see me, are you not, Cat?" He produced deer jerky from an inner fold of his thick garments, but the Lynx, truly enthralled by him, ignored it.

"My Lord," Sage bowed her head and curtsied before him.

Merlin stood, stepped forward and embraced her. She then looked in his sparkly blue eyes and was immediately reminded of Artos. It looked like there were stars in his eyes.

"Draigathar! What pleasure to behold you. It seems that I have been summoned," at this he raised his bushy white eyebrows, and his eye twinkled, "so I wasted no time and came speedily."

"Yes, sir; do you know Her Highness Dark Star MacLeod of Caithness?"

A smile crept over Merlin's face. "Ah, that tattooed cat woman! *She* is here? Causing all sorts of mischief, to be sure?"

It took Sage a few moments to realize he spoke in jest. *He is not so formidable as I thought...it is possible to be calm before this man,* she thought inwardly. But she replied: "Indeed Dark Star is here, in Avalon—under this very roof, my Lord. I shall wake her, and the Lady Morgan."

This action was not necessary, as by this point both of those women, awakened by the noise, entered the room. Sage wondered how Dark Star could look so regal, freshly woken in the middle of the night. The tattoos on her neck writhed in the firelight. She glided towards Merlin, extending her paws, as she exclaimed: "Such a lively ruckus! I should have known *you* were behind it!" The two embraced, and after, they stared at each other, Merlin holding Dark Star's paws in his hands.

"Lady, time does not change you," he uttered adoringly. He then turned to Morgan. They bowed to each other, clearly relieved to see each other. She handed him a vessel of

Avalon's mead. "And Morgan, how does Avalon? I see you are in the highest of company—I wonder for what reason you could need an old man like me!" Again his twilight blue eyes twinkled away.

They all sat down and the Lynx sat right at Merlin's feet, looking up at him reverently, muzzle in the air. He continued his powerful purring, and it was an auspicious sound for the meeting at hand. Merlin grew suddenly serious, and looked them all in the eye. "You wish to speak to me of Axis."

Dark Star raised her brows, causing her crown of emeralds to lift, and her star tattoo to crinkle. Then she smiled. "So you know her," she purred.

"I have known her for at least forever...for eternities; she and I have walked infinity together...her task in this life is very difficult. She has no physical teacher, no high spirit companions, as we have, here," he gestured towards all in the room. He continued, running his hand through his beard. "Her task is to Remember: to remember us, remember Avalon, remember herself as a shaman, for that is what she has been in so many lives. I have been sending her ever so many messages, all of her life. It has taken many years for her to become unblinded enough to decipher my messages. I have come to her as a pig, a hawk, a stag, a dragonfly. Most recently I came to her as a snake. I have visited her dreams as a mountain lion, as a horse, as a faerie. She understands at first—then within hours she doubts herself, doubts me, us, Avalon...it has been very difficult. But now I must happily announce that she has opened a conscious door of communication between us—with me—and we have been sending messages to each other quite regularly."

He gazed at them all, and his eyes were so sharp they sliced through the very air.

Sage summoned her courage, inhaled deeply, and addressed Merlin. "Then, it stands to reason, that...you know Wyrrd."

He cocked his head and regarded her with a questioning gaze.

"The Maiden Wyrrd—she is a sister here at Avalon—right now—and she shares the same soul as does Axis," Sage explained.

"Wyrrd—she is young, yes? I knew of her presence in life, but as of yet, I have not made her acquaintance."

Dark Star interjected. "That is a brilliant point well made, Sage." She turned toward Merlin. "Here is why we summoned you. Sage went to see Axis, using the Cards of the Chalice. Axis told her she needs proof, something tangible of the existence of Avalon, so that the people of her time will believe that it truly exists. I thought perhaps you could help us; someone must go between the worlds, and who is more adept than you? Axis can't come here; even if she could get here by dreamwalking, I know she would never want to go back. Then she would die, and would not be able to fulfill her mission."

"True, true," expressed Merlin. "Let me guess, you want me to make a special delivery? What would it be? A cattail, an apple branch, a vessel of water from the sacred well? And it would have to be unmistakable, or else she would doubt its authenticity."

After a brief silence, Morgan spoke. "Wait. The fact is that Avalon will never die. Just as the truth never dies. Avalon is the truth. Should it not just be as it is now, that only those with magical minds can enter?"

Dark Star purred in reply. "Your point is sound, sister, but for what else are we here? If people can't come to the magic, then the magic must go to the people. They must open their eyes, yes. And some will be forever blind. But I believe this is something we should attempt. Merlin: are you willing? To go between the worlds and through time, to deliver a piece of Avalon?"

"Before I commit to such a thing, first I would like to meet the young lady, the maiden, Wyrrd. I am sure she can help me." He waited, pondering, fingers pressed to his lips. Then: "There is only one way for this to work. Axis has to believe that it can happen. She has to know that it is really true, that a physical object can be brought through fifteen hundred years. Or else I can not do it."

He continued. "You see, doubt has always been her biggest adversary. As we know, doubt is the killer of magic. Part of Axis's destiny is to let go of doubt, and know the reality of magic, in her heart and the world. Until she does that, I can not deliver what she wants."

He rose. "I will be meditating in a private place for the next twenty four hours. Then I will return. At that time I wish to have an audience with the maiden Wyrrd." Bowing his adieu, he exited readily, out into the dark of the night.

Nine

MERLIN MEETS AXIS

After taking in the exquisite smelling night air, Merlin arrived at the Gateway Tree. The air had revived him. It was full of aromas; some nameless, some named, that bespoke of its very own wisdom. The earthy smell of leaves decaying; an almost balmy sweetness borne of fall; somehow the air itself was a teacher, and its smells spoke soothingly. With each inhalation Merlin felt the truth of the world, of magic, enter him. By the time he reached the Gateway Tree he was very calmed.

Axis. What was he to do? He could not force her destiny; he could not deliver to her some thing, an apple perhaps, and think that she had learned the lesson. The lesson being that of remembrance itself; once Axis remembered her own ancient powers enough, she would very well know exactly how to conduct this experiment.

Truth be told, he was thrilled she was finally at this stage. How long he had been sending her messages! But it was his way to send them coded (he was the ultimate trickster), and they needed deciphering. Only recently had she begun understanding the cryptic messages, stored within visions, which he had been sending her. He sent them psychically, usually while she was asleep.

Now I will send her a new one, he thought. It was very simple: *Listen to the trees.* He crawled into the opening of the hollow Gateway Tree, his dark purple robes trailing the ground. Here he sat in meditation, directing force fields of energy towards the psyche of Axis, and when he finally felt himself lock on, merged with her spirit and soul, he chanted an inward incantation: *Listen to the trees. Consult the Oracle. The trees are older than people, older than animals. Especially the conifers.* Merlin sent this message, along with vibrations of magic that defy definition, through time and through space and between the folds of the worlds, and he continued until he knew it had reached its destination.

It will be a whole new kind of listening for her, he thought. Then he slept upon the moss, curled in the base of the Gateway Tree.

By morning, and after sleep, Merlin had become eager to meet Wyrrd. While her soul and Merlin's soul were deeply bonded, it had been a long time, perhaps centuries, since the two had been together in physical form. But he knew not to expect too much; she was young; he knew not to expect her to *remember*. Still, something told him she might be quite extraordinary.

On winged feet he accelerated to the dwelling of Morgan. She, Dark Star, and Sage were engaged in their morning meditation, and he interrupted them only briefly, with this message: "Tell her to meet me at the base of the apple tree on the edge of the lake, the one with nine stones surrounding it." With that he was gone.

Wyrrd had been instructed to meet Merlin at Morgan's, and when she arrived there, she had Shoonach. While Shoonach and the Lynx sniffed each other, surprisingly courteously, the women fussed over Wyrrd. They smoothed her long reddish locks, adjusted her gold neckpiece, and brushed the velvet of her skirts.

"Do be aware, Lady, that you know this man. As he puts it, he has known you 'for at least forever...for eternities; she and I have walked infinity together.' Still, you will do well to calm yourself deeply before seeing him, so that you might connect with the memory..."

Morgan smiled at Wyrrd and gave her a warm embrace. "Do not be nervous, sister. You will love him!" She went on, in her warbling, deep voice: "Breathe deeply, don't forget that, and align with the very core of who you are. That is your soul. Within that core you are also Axis."

They ushered her out the door, sending her on her way to the apple tree on the edge. Shoonach stayed behind with the Lynx. Something started to happen to Wyrrd on the way to the tree. The only way for her to describe it was that it felt like Axis was coming into her body. Since they shared the same soul, it was not a bad feeling; rather, it helped with her alignment. She felt more solid as a result of it. She felt more power. With each inhalation of the sweet fresh air, she felt more strong. By the time she reached Merlin, she was quite transformed. She saw an old man seated on a stone at the base of the apple tree. He wore purple robes and had long silver hair, and vibrated the unmistakable energy of sovereignty.

The trunk of the apple tree grew out of a mossy bluff which descended to the lake. Surrounding the tree were nine big stones, somewhat grown over with lichen. The tree was laden with apples, most green, some turning reddish. At the very bottom where the trunk met moss, the trunk had grown an appendage: it looked like a reclining stag with its head up, and antlers. The tips of the antlers had leaves growing out of them.

Wyrrd stood in front of the man, bowed her head, and whispered, "My Lord Merlin." It was so obvious to her now, that she already knew him, she almost began to cry. The cry would have been of remembrance, of ancientness; of joy at being reunited with one of her eternal best friends. Discipline enabled her to check her tears, though not before Merlin saw the glazed over moisture in her eyes. He knew the same cry. The same thing happened to him. At last, he spoke. "Lady. Finally." This was all he said, but he said it in such a way, in a certain hushed tone, and the words sunk in: they spoke of eternities waiting to see someone, and of missing her.

"You are so young!" he then expostulated, as if to suggest he thought she would be ancient. He stared into her eyes, into her soul, and it seemed that someone else was looking at him, and he knew it was Axis. "It is such a way of magic, what the Great Spirit does, in creating multiple facets for the same soul. Each facet has its own beauties, its own pure uniqueness, and its own brand of love. This is part of the unknowable, how the Great Spirit can do this; can chip off endless facets of itself, all as stunning as diamonds."

Wyrrd nodded, in amazement and agreement. She knew what he meant, but not in a way she could ever explain. Now it seemed her mind clouded over. She heard herself begin to speak, but the words were not hers, nor was the language, nor the accent or voice: "O my King, my god, my best friend! O Merlin. It feels it has taken forever for me to be back with you!"

Merlin understood it all perfectly. "My blessed Lady! What may I do for you? I understand that you want something to be brought between the worlds, to unveil in your country, as proof....sure I am not, yet, how we would do this." And then he looked at her cryptically, staring straight into her pupil. "Though knowing you, I know you will find the way."

"But for now, sit! Sit under this beautiful tree with me, sit upon a stone, and breathe the fresh morning air."

The body of the Maiden Wyrrd, holding the spirit of Axis, sat upon the big rock next to Merlin. She was quite in heaven. She smiled serenely, and tilted her head sideways as she gazed upon him. "Aye, sir. I am ascending to my destiny. And you are part of that destiny. You and I, we have always been together. Life before I remembered you has been so empty...now I know you tried diligently to present yourself, to awaken memory in me—and so many times you came to me and you were invisible. Really it was that I, as Axis, could not see you. It was because I was blind! But now, now that I have meditated and purified myself through the fog, I see you again. I know your signs, your cryptic messages."

"What you have done to get here...this is different than dreamwalking... how did you do it?"

Axis smiled triumphantly. "I created a tunnel through time. Or maybe it was always there, and I just had to find it. Once found, this tunnel has been my method, my pathway, and I have traveled my spirit upon it, to meet with you."

"So you never lost your faerie blood," Merlin breathed softly.

"It is not possible for faerie blood to be completely diluted. A strain of it lasts forever. Once a soul obtains faerie blood, the soul always has it, through every lifetime. It is this magical blood which has helped me reawaken my memory. But of course you know such things!"

Axis stood up and began walking in sunwise circles around the tree, within the ring of nine stones. She bent down and removed her boots (Wyrrd's boots). "Ah! Moss upon the feet! How I have missed this!"

"Is there not moss in your country, Lady?"

"Oh, there is, but one must seek it out. This is such a luscious big patch!" She continued her walk. "Merlin, I've come to realize that I know the language of moss, of lichen, and of insects. I have felt moss welcoming me as a long lost friend. And with insects—I do not believe there are human words for how to translate the language. But

I receive their messages as feelings, non human feelings..."

"You are just very old, Lady. Insects were living upon the earth even before there were trees...and mosses were living upon the earth far before there were insects...you have an ancient soul."

Axis touched the bark of the tree. She rested her hand there, and looked at Merlin. He was sitting on his rock, so sweetly and kindly, and she was touched by how gentle he was.

"What of magic?" Axis began. "What of Avalon? It is my destiny to bring Avalon back to the people, so they may know magic again, know magic exists—that in fact it was *always* there, has always been here, never left..."

"First you must realize," and now Merlin's voice had the touch of authority, "First you must realize that *your* country is the lost world, and Avalon is reality. For so long you have thought it was the reverse. Know this: Avalon is not lost. Magic is not lost. These things are the truth, and the truth never dies. It is that dense world that you have come from, that dense future alternate reality, somehow existing on earth, that is very lost. By lost I mean, lost from goodness, from righteousness, from love, from magic. It is a world that is heavily influenced by priests who know very little of the true Jesus Christ. Jesus is, was, and will always be God, and if God is one thing, God is love."

Tears welled up in Axis's eyes. Merlin spoke again. "The place where you live—it is a bad dream, a nightmare. There are some good places, some righteous spots, some kind people. But on the whole, it is a place of dysfunction, where evils such as murder, incest, rape and greed are commonplace. Greed for money, the false sense of power, seems to have taken over that world. You can't possibly view a world like that as reality. The best thing you can do is contrive waking from that bad dream."

She looked directly into his violet pupils and knew what he said was exactly true. "Merlin, I want to go to a place where there is only truth. Where I am surrounded by trees; I want to go to ancient forests that are so dense and hidden that people don't even know they exist."

He smiled kindly. "The forests of which you speak—they are just across the folds of this world. Only a magic-minded person could enter. There are roads that lead in between the worlds, and you can find them." His eyes sparkled at her. Little waves of the lake lapped the mossy bank. The beating of wings in the air caused them to look up, and there in the sky was a great owl, rare in daylight. It flew across the sun.

"Well, that settles it. I must take you to the ancient forests. Better yet—you are in need of a male consort. It will be balancing and healing for you. But first, you will have to allow Wyrrd her own mind back, if only for a short time. I need to make sure your entry is not causing her harm in any way."

"So I will retreat, and when I come back, you will introduce me to a male consort? Tell me, Merlin—do you know of MacTail of Carmarthen?"

He waved his right hand gently in a gesture of dismissal, not answering. But as Axis faded from Wyrrd's mind, she thought she saw a glimmer of knowing in Merlin's blue eye.

Ten

MACTAIL OF CARMARTHEN AND THE HIDDEN FOREST

When Axis's psyche re-entered Wyrrd's mind, the first thing she heard was Merlin's voice. She felt an animal beneath her and realized she was seated upon a horse. Ahead of her the world looked more different than ever; beauty was different upon the trees, edges were softer, and everything—sky, earth, and all growth—had a golden glow.

She heard Merlin's voice before even turning sideways to look at him. He was saying, "and it may not be easy. I am warning you. He is very handsome. I am warning you in advance not to swoon. The point of your meeting MacTail is that you are ready for him, ready for this type of spiritual balance.

This is not a romance. You are to be consorts, best friends if you like—but no romance." And with that he shot her a hawk-like glance.

Axis suppressed a giggle. He was so serious! *If only he knew how relieved I am to not have romance. That's the last kind of trouble I need right now,* she thought. Instead of giggling she nodded her head solemnly, and changed the subject: "How does Wyrrd, Lord?"

"It seems that your intrusion had virtually no effect on her! After you departed, she blinked, looked at me, and said, 'What was it you were saying, Merlin? Forgive me; I seem to have drifted in my thoughts.' So I am not worried about her, and Dark Star knows she is with me—us. Just keep her well fed and watered, will you?" He smiled.

The horses trod along towards the edge of a wood. The trees looked immensely tall, their evergreenness thick and lush. "Now you will see what I mean about there being roads in between the worlds. Close your eyes, and let your horse lead you. Horses know the way. Keep your eyes closed! Now listen to me. The next time you open your eyes I will be gone. You will find MacTail, and he will know what to do. Remember to bring Wyrrd back to Avalon. MacTail will help you, he knows of these things. And remember: no swooning! My Lady, I bid you adieu and soothing travels."

Axis knew not to open her eyes, and she smiled her farewell. She heard Merlin's horse's hooves moving further and further away. Still she kept her eyes closed. She tapped her heels against her horse's belly, and it began to walk decisively. Now she was in total trust of her horse, a horse she did not even know.

With closed eyes, sounds and smells are stronger. The sharp and sweet green pine scent permeated the air. With each inhalation she grew more relaxed, to the point of a deep balanced bliss. There was wind whistling through the treetops, and multitudes of small birds fluttered and flew all about in her vicinity, their wingbeats vibrating the scented air. *I wish I could stay here forever,* Axis thought. Occasional shafts of sunlight broke through the moving tree boughs, splashing her face with warmth.

Was she on a road? She did not want to open her eyes to find out. The feeling of the world was different, though. *This must be a faerie land,* she thought. Now she heard little voices, or thought she did. She would no sooner hear a little chortle, than it would be gone and she would doubt that she had really heard it. *It must have been the wind,* she thought.

But then Axis heard a loud, deep man's voice. "Hi Ho, My Lady!"

And she opened her eyes. There he was: it was MacTail of Carmarthen, who had been coming to her in dreams. He was huge. He was a big man on a big horse, with a decorated breastplate bearing his family's coat of arms. The breastplate was red and blue, and had silver symbols of dragons. There was a sword hanging by his side, and even from a distance the hilt of it was visibly laden with red and blue jewels. His horse pawed the ground. Axis finally looked into the face of MacTail of Carmarthen. There was no more handsome man. There were no more shining blue eyes. There was no higher smile, no whiter teeth, redder lips, thicker hair. He was a god.

MacTail leaped from his horse and landed soundly upon the forest floor. He strode to Axis's side, and lifted her from her horse in one swift movement. He was very strong. "Lady," he murmured, and picked up a lock of her hair, which he pulled forward, forward enough for her to see that it was blond. "I knew you would still have blond hair."

Axis was startled. He was looking at her *own* hair—not Wyrrd's reddish locks. "What color are my eyes, my Lord?"

"Green," and his voice rumbled like thunder.

But Wyrrd's eyes were also green, so Axis looked down at her clothes and hands. It was true: they were *her* clothes, and *her* hands, from fifteen hundred years away, not Wyrrd's long velvet draperies. Somehow she had regained herself; she had entered this secret forest, and become her true, whole self, without the help of Wyrrd or her body or mind. *So it really is me with MacTail then,* she thought.

With the confidence born of being her whole and true self, Axis looked boldly into the eyes of MacTail. Her lips broke into a wide smile, as though being reunited with a long lost love or family member. MacTail eyed her playfully. "You called?" he smiled as he spoke.

Axis sighed in bliss and relief. She stared into his pupils, which themselves looked like gateways to other lands. "I am so happy, my smile is at the beginning of eternity." She paused, still staring at him. "You are a magic man."

"I'm actually your male counterpart. As in, we complete each other."

"And we are to be best friends, yes?"

"My Lady, we are best friends already, always have been, always will be. What troubles you?" MacTail said with such kindness, it melted her heart and she had to hold back her tears.

"The world in which I live—oh my Lord, it is dreadful. It is full of negative, bothersome, unwholesome things, not to mention evil and noise and pollution, murder and incest, extraordinary greed, dishonesty, adultery, unconsciousness, egocentrism, arrogance and ignorance. I am so miserable living there! It is such hard work to focus on the good, when I am forever being distracted by the bad! I am literally surrounded by unconsciousness. The only thing that keeps me sane is my daily meditations, and plants and animals. And I feel guilty for being miserable. When will I ever wake from this dream? It is too much for my fragile mind to bear."

At this, he hugged her. She was not swooning, not at all: she was being honest, not pretending that everything was perfect in order to put on an agreeable face. "MacTail— where are we? Where is this place?"

"There are veils between the worlds. The different veils protect certain worlds, like this one, from intruders. For example, the only people who could enter this forest would be people we would want to see. Like Merlin, Morgan, Dark Star."

Axis's eyes got wide. "I knew you would know Dark Star! I just knew it!"

MacTail smiled and continued: "If I could slice through this veil with my sword, the Welsh city of Carmarthen would be right on the on the other side of it." He looked at her pondering face.

"Do not try to understand it. That is why mystery is mystery, and magic is magic. What would life be, if there were no secrets?"

"I can not believe that a city is right next to us. I do not want to be near a city, MacTail. I want to be as far away from all that as possible."

"And that you are, Lady. We are truly far away, because we are truly in another world. Only magic minded people can enter. That is why you are here. Do you know, I have been waiting for you for such a long time, such a very long time?"

"You must have faerie blood as well then, yes?"

MacTail reached out and gently stroked her cheek. "I do. You know, I need you as much as you need me."

"You do? Why?" The moisture in the air glistened on her pale pink cheeks, making her eyes appear more green than ever.

"Why? You need to ask? Because we have been displaced from each other, oh so long ago. You were sent to the future to bring about your particular destiny. Do you not remember, Lady, my Axis? Do you not remember all of our times together in history?"

"I do...only it is foggy, blurry....I certainly do not remember events. More so I remember a kinship, a companionship, which lives on in me as a feeling. I only know that I have craved you—not so much as a husband or a romance—but mostly as my companion and best friend."

"That is what I meant about our being counterparts. Now then. Let us relish our time in this utopian forest. Let us go to glades of moss, where I have a tree so giant you can live in it, which I know you will love."

Her eyes wide, Axis kept silent. MacTail placed her back upon her horse, leaped onto his, and the horses walked together, deeper and deeper into the ancient forest. How did Axis know it was ancient? She could feel it. The trees felt like they had been there forever. She heard Merlin's voice: *Listen to the trees. Especially the conifers.* There was no better place than here to do just that. The pinecones hanging from boughs, and lying upon the earth, waved in the wind and were as giant as a man's thigh. The gentle winds and breezes made music with the trees, as if the trees were their instruments. It was a different language than that of humans, and in her deep calmness at being here with MacTail, Axis intended to decipher it. What did it say? First, she was being welcomed. The tree language spoke to a part of her mind that had never heard language before.

Amongst the silences of the wood, the horse's hooves rustled the pine needles of the forest floor. The bark of the trees had faces. At first she thought she was imagining it, but after a time Axis realized that she really could see faces in the trees, and they were the faces of the tree's spirits. One looked exactly like a lion.

MacTail and Axis trod over well worn paths. Axis wanted to ask about the paths but preferred her silence. Feelings of deep safety permeated her whole spirit. The crisp, cool air kept filtering through her nostrils, purifying her body. The sound of an owl's call came so suddenly and so close, Axis almost jumped. "Hoo-hoo-hoo!" The owl was close by, and Axis could see it. She pointed, to show MacTail, but he was already looking at it. The owl was sitting upright on a horizontal branch, its sharp yellow eyes staring at them.

This world felt so much more saturated with realness than the future world from which she had come. Again she attempted to listen to the trees, to understand their messages. She understood that these trees were in charge. They had power. It was so much different than human power; it felt God-driven. By being amongst them, now she was part of that gigantic power. It waved by her, around her, within her. These trees had no fear. There was no fear in the whole forest. Axis knew why: it was not possible for humans to chop down this forest, because this world was completely displaced from linear human reality. The only humans who could find this place would be part human faeries, like herself and MacTail, and they would never harm it. *Oh, I would that I never had to go back to my old life!* she mused.

Axis looked over at MacTail, who was on her right. His blue eyes rested on hers questioningly; he smiled with his mouth closed, a slow smile. He looked completely content. She tried to imagine him being in her other world. *Women would die for him,* she thought.

She began to realize that the trees were their own race. Each tree had its own personality and soul, just like people, but higher. As it happens with people, there are some we are more attracted to than others. Axis began to notice that she felt a certain magnetic attraction towards some trees, while others did not affect her as strongly, and some even felt imposing. *At some point, one of these trees will be my friend,* she thought.

They neared a glade. Moss was everywhere, and it had its own language too. It was welcoming, sending its energy out in tendrils, beckoning them to sit upon it. Enclosing the glade on one side was the most colossal tree Axis had ever seen. Its diameter was at least twelve feet across. *I* could *live in this tree!* Axis thought with joy. She descended her mount by herself, so eager was she to touch the tree. By the time she reached it, a large opening was visible in one side of its trunk. She spread her arms as wide as possible and pressed them and her body against the tree. The tree was humble, she could sense that.

Sunlight played upon the glittering moss, and it sparkled like a sea of emeralds. MacTail dismounted, and walked over to Axis, pointing at the tree opening. He leaned over and walked inside! Axis followed him. They were both inside the tree, standing up. It was light in there, due to some holes left from fallen branches which filtered in sunlight. Moss blanketed the ground. There were two rocks inside the tree, nestled into the moss, and the moss had grown up around their edges. MacTail gestured to the rocks, and he and Axis sat down. The rocks were perfect seats.

Axis wanted to say something, anything, but she was struck silent. What was there to say? It was the single most perfect experience of her entire life. It was made even more perfect by an unexpected visitor. A little squirrel scurried inside of the tree. It looked at Axis, then MacTail; then back at Axis. It ran laps around the circumference of the interior, and finally came and began sniffing Axis's legs. Ever so slowly she extended a hand. The squirrel sniffed her hand, and she ached to touch the fur. The squirrel looked up into her eyes, and it did not look scared. Axis touched its fur. The squirrel was so wiggly that its body kept vibrating, but it let Axis pet it. In that moment Axis forgot about every single thing on earth, even MacTail.

She cupped her hand to see if the squirrel could be scooped up. *If I can pick up this squirrel, it will be too good to be true!* Axis thought fleetingly. And she did. The squirrel allowed itself to be picked up, and elevated into Axis's lap. It was the most adorable thing Axis had ever held. It wiggled and moved constantly, sniffing her palms and fingers, its round black eyes looking up into her face.

The fur was so soft, and the tail so bushy. Finally, after a minute the squirrel, of its own accord, jumped down to the moss. It glanced back at MacTail, took one last look at Axis and darted out the opening of the tree.

"It is amazing how the presence of a sweet little animal can put me at peace," Axis said to MacTail.

"I agree. Not everyone feels such a way about animals, but I do. They have such bright spirits. They make the best do with everything. I often think they are much happier than people, because they lead simple lives."

"Yes my Lord, for example, a little squirrel is not pacing to and fro before her wardrobe each morning, deciding which gown to wear!"

MacTail became serious in demeanor. "I am heartened to see you using humor, my Lady. Because it is evident from your earlier words that you are often sad. You have to stop feeling sorry for yourself. You chose your destiny! You designed it with your very own soul! You must start understanding why you chose this destiny. Always you must remember that this is real—this forest, this tree—me—and I am here for you always."

She had been staring at the tree's walls, the soft interior wood. There were many grooves and channels that insects had carved, that looked like meandering rivers. He was right. She thought, *I must stop feeling sorry for myself.*

"But it is so hard, MacTail. You do not know what I endure, being part faerie, aware of magic, surrounded by pure humans who know absolutely nothing of this. It is hard to make friends—everyone is so false!"

"Yes but again—you chose this. And a spirit never chooses something it can not endure. Perhaps you would do well to employ the characteristic of solemnity. That means that you sit in the place of awe, and you are aware of the sublime. Solemnity is a sacred state. It is difficult to be distracted by common disturbances if you practice being solemn. Think of Dark Star. She has taken solemnity to the heights."

"Then I must be more aware of that which is sublime."

Sometimes nature hears people talking. MacTail and Axis, having been inside the tree for some time now, were unaware of how much the sky had changed. Storm clouds had moved in, and thunder began to rumble. The sound of it precluded any further speech from Axis, and she stared up at the holes that looked outside. All she could see was green. Thunder came again, this time louder. Axis rose and turned and exited the tree opening.

The forest floor shook and was lit up with white light. She stood on the moss bed and stared up at the sky, and all the while the thunder became louder and louder. It was reaching a pinnacle. Zigzag lightning bolts reached toward earth. Then came her glory: a crack so loud she thought she would be deafened; a crack so loud her jaw dropped and tears came to her eyes. There was no doubt, absolutely no doubt in all the universes who was really in charge. It was God. The thunder did not scare her, rather, it was sublime. It was the highest of the high. Nothing could be above it. Then there came another deafening crack, a crack so loud it sounded like it could rip the sky and world apart. But it was a voice, and Axis knew that it was the voice of God.

It purified her. It pushed all thoughts, worries, and concerns into oblivion. Nothing else could be heard, as the thunder continued. Axis did have one thought: *I wish that I could hear this every day.* In answer the thunder rumbled again. It was her language, just as it was Sage's language, Wyrrd's language, Dark Star's. If anything could bring on the height of solemnity, it was this.

Axis was still standing, with her bare feet enmeshed in the moss, her face upturned to the sky, when the first raindrops fell upon her face. She did not know that MacTail was standing right behind her, in the same position.

"We are the Thunder People," he whispered softly. "We give our lives to the thunder, and the thunder teaches us. It is our god, above all others."

Once Axis was full of thunder, it began to soften. Only lessening rumbles were heard now, caressing her ears and soul. She turned and looked up at MacTail's face. He said one thing: "It knows." And he embraced her. The rain began; she pulled herself away, and went back into the tree. Here she curled on the moss floor, and slept.

Eleven

OF DRAGONS AND DESTINY

The sun was shining when Axis walked out of the tree. MacTail was seated within the glade, upon the green glittering moss, evergreen trees framing him. While taken aback by how handsome he was, Merlin's voice played in her mind: *And remember: no swooning!* If she hadn't felt such a deep level of security and companionship with MacTail, perhaps Merlin's concerns would have been valid. But Axis was so fulfilled by the alliance as it was, there was no need for her to fantasize that it were any different.

His blue eyes sent beams towards her, so thick they were almost tangible.

"MacTail, let us walk through the forest—I am craving exercise," she announced, tilting her head sideways in her customary way and smiling sweetly.

He was vertical in an instant. *I can not believe how big he is,* Axis thought. "Why does your breastplate bear dragons?"

They began walking.

"My family, the clan Carmarthen, always has believed in magic, even when magic moved further and further away from the world of men. The dragon is an alchemic animal, able to fly, swim, and breathe fire. My forefathers thought the dragon so magical, they chose this animal as the family symbol." He smiled proudly, his perfect white teeth showing. Sparks like stars danced in his eyes.

"Have you ever seen one, Lord?"

"I have and it was guarding the face of a barrow. It was twisted and curled, and when it sensed me, it opened its eyes and looked right at me. Do I need to say that there is nothing more frightening, nothing more awe-inspiring, nothing more spellbinding than to lock eyes with a dragon? But after a few moments, it blinked—blinked big shimmering green lids, and it kept blinking, and I could feel it was a welcoming message. The dragon was docile with my presence, and it let me stare at it. I stared at its glinting rainbow scales, as they refracted light. If it moved one inch, it was like a swirling kaleidoscope. Finally, it closed its eyes, and as the eyelids sealed shut I could tell that I was then separate from its world. I stared for only a few moments longer and out of respect I then departed."

"Where did you see this animal?" The walk was doing them good, Axis becoming more and more exuberant with each step.

"In a world such as this. A world no pure humans could enter. That is why pure humans do not believe in dragons, they think they are strictly imaginary creatures."

Axis was swinging her arms to and fro as they walked. "I am so grateful to have faerie blood. Without it surely I could not survive the human world."

"Without it, Lady, you would not have your particular destiny. Faeries are always being given these extraordinary tasks, such as yours. If you could define it briefly, in one sentence, how would you describe your destiny?"

"To bring Avalon back."

"Back to—where? What does that mean?"

Axis looked sidelong at him and raised her eyebrow high. "That is what I am to find out. First of all, it has to be made more accessible to the human world so they can no longer deny that magic exists."

"And then..."

"And then, I began realizing that..." her voice trailed off. She walked and breathed and smelled the crisp sweet pine scent. She stopped briefly to pick up an especially enormous pinecone. "Look at this! If I did not see this with my very own eyes, I would not believe it was possible!" She gently touched the pods of the pinecone, and placed it back exactly where it had been. They kept walking, in and amongst the trees, and MacTail looked at her, expectantly.

"I began realizing that Avalon is not lost. Rather, humanity lost touch with the path that leads to it. So, for those who want to know, and who have a craving; for those who are open minded to the subtlety of magic—I must share my experiences and memories. As has been said to me before: The Truth Never Dies."

She paused, reflecting. "First Sage did work, by opening up the global mind, and it was an awesome advancement. But I must accept that it could take one thousand more years before humanity is so open to magic that they can really see Avalon again. But what is one thousand years, my Lord? There are trees three times that old, and rocks a billion times older. But let us hope it does not take that long. I will share my discoveries, and pray that the more thick human belief becomes, the more visible and tangible Avalon will become again...it is like a *quickening*...and thus Avalon will be back in the human world."

"In what manner do you plan to expose your experiences and memories?"

"In the form of a story, a book..."

"What will you call it?"

"Why, *Bringing Avalon Back*, of course."

By now they were standing in a glade. The sun was shining down, and a circle of trees enclosed them. MacTail smiled down at Axis—she was so much shorter—in a loving, kind way. Axis beamed up at him.

"You should be very proud, Lady, of pursuing such a destiny."

"I am. It is so hard sometimes, what with the distractions of my world. But I can not deny this destiny. It makes me feel like I am going to the absolute limits of what is possible, and that gives me a pure feeling of freedom."

"But I miss Merlin, MacTail, and I greatly need to be near him."

"Well then, that shall be arranged. Let us send him messages tonight. The moon will be perfect for it." MacTail pointed upwards. The new moon hung in the sky like a smile. From the perspective of Avalon, that is the most magical moon.

While still in the glade, with the sun shining upon them, a perfectly formed oak leaf appeared in the middle of the air. Axis just saw it suddenly; it did not seem to originate from a certain place. It seemed, rather, to have been born within the very air. And then it descended. So obvious was it that the leaf was for her that she extended her open hand, until the leaf rested gently there. It was an older leaf, rather brown, like a leaf fallen in autumn.

Axis looked at MacTail and for a moment their locked eyes shared the experience of solemnity. They both knew who sent the leaf, but still Axis spoke: "It's from Merlin."

"Merlin will always be with you. You have to *know* that," said MacTail urgently. "Meditate upon him, think of him, wonder about him. This will keep him alive in you." Then, as if suddenly remembering something, he began again: "He will always come to you, sending you messages, even when it seems you have forgotten him."

Upon further reflection, MacTail said to Axis: "This book that you are writing about Avalon—it's a spell. *The book itself is a spell.* As the book gets read, the thread that ties Avalon to the future will thicken. This is what you have brought between the worlds—by linking yourself to our voices, and giving us freedom upon the page. Within your book we can do whatever we want. Is it so?"

I nodded. I, who am Axis, nodded my assent. Spirits come to us in dreams and through the air, and it is our job to be receptive. If we are open enough, then we can give purer voice to these spirits of our past, who are still trying to teach us the great, nameless lessons of God.

Twelve

DARK STAR AND THE PEARL

Dark Star sat in her chamber. She stared into the shimmers of the pearl in the brooch on the purple pouch. Sometimes in the shimmers she could see things, other worlds. This time she could see Axis. It seemed that Axis was staring straight at her through the pearl. *How can she be looking at me through the pearl?* Dark Star wondered. *What is it she stares at? Such that she can see right through it?*

Then Dark Star saw something else. Eyes.

Sage arrived. Dark Star, holding the pouch and gesturing to the pearl, said: "I keep feeling like someone strange is staring at us. I see eyes. It must be the reader."

"The reader?"

"We're in a book. Axis has written a book about us, so of course people can see us."

"You mean the people who are reading the book. Can see us." Sage sounded slightly disgruntled.

"Yes. That is how books work. You have privacy most of the time, but in certain situations, if the event is described in detail, you can be seen."

"But, we are real!"

"Yes, Sage, some books are about real people and real things that are occurring. Don't worry, most of the time your thoughts are private. The readers usually don't have access to our thoughts, unless Axis exposes them, which she does only occasionally."

Dark Star, staring out the window, suddenly had an idea. "I'm speaking to them!" she announced to Sage.

Sage looked alarmed. "Lady, how...and what would you say?"

"How? Through this pearl, of course. I'm going to look right through it, into their eyes, and it's the words, you see, the words act as conduits...They see us through the words. I see their eyes through this pearl. The words are like tunnels."

After a time: "And what would you say?"

"I don't know yet. I must ponder upon it." She rested a leopard paw upon her forehead, its fur obscuring her tattoo. Somehow, there was something magical about the cat paw upon the inked star, and magic began to brew...

"The reader must become part of the magic spell."

And then: "The lineage of Avalon has never stopped through all these centuries, right into the future century Axis inhabits. It is a lineage of blood and faerie strain. And it will not die, because it is the truth. If I can just find a way to give the person reading this a glimpse of Avalon..." With her paw still upon her forehead, she stared off into space.

"There is a secret passageway to Avalon, and it would be accessible to the reader by my means. But s/he would have to follow me." Here Dark Star pauses one last time, and takes in a deep solemn breath. "Right, Sage, the moment has arrived: I will now address the reader." Dark Star looks into the pearl, and she sees you (yes, you, the person reading this).

Dark Star bows to you. You hear her otherworldly purr, and the language does not sound like English, but you understand it anyway: "Greetings. If you follow me I will guide you, and then you can come here too. Come, travel this tunnel with me." You see her big solemn eyes.

You walk. There are leopard skins on the walls, and ancient petroglyphs. The ceiling is low. The air smells prehistoric. The molecules of the air are old because this tunnel was built before the beginning of time.

Dark Star slows, turns around and looks at you.

It's she. Her brown eyes look right into yours, and above them you see her black diamond star tattoo with the emerald head band across her forehead.

She purrs: "Do not be scared. You do not have to come if you don't want to. But by reading this you are coming. Words are magic; words are part of this tunnel. These words have woven a spell. And if you do not want to follow me, then you must stop reading now."

She soothingly looks at you. Who would not want to follow?

"You are safe, as long as you are with me, so come along," she beckons, waving her paw forward in the air.

She turns and moves further along the tunnel. You follow her black velvet draperies.

Where is the light coming from? From her torch. From it you see gemstones inlaid in the walls themselves. Then you see coats of arms, red and blue with silver dragons. Does it look familiar? This is the heraldry of MacTail of Carmarthen.

The air is becoming thick with something like incense. The scent is sandalwood; it is warm and embracing, enveloping. You are enfolded and suddenly Dark Star turns one last corner and you practically bump into her, because she has stopped in an antechamber.

Here are Sage, and the Lynx, and MacTail, and Axis. Here are Morgan and

Merlin. Fire lights the walls, and there is a window on the far side of the room.

Axis looks right at you. She is the Norwegian beauty, with a crown of spiral shells and jagged coral on her head, with long blond hair and green eyes. "Do you want to be part of the beginning?" she asks you directly, in modern English.

You don't know what this means, and that is all right.

There is a crucifix on the wall, and on it, Jesus is still alive. Do not try to figure it out; you can not. You look in Jesus's eyes. He is so small at first, just hanging on the wall there. Then He takes over the room with His eyes. His eyes perform some magic trick, in which they are all you see.

Now you are looking into Jesus's eyes. You can hear his language and it is at once Aramaic and simultaneously being translated into English as it enters your ears. You hear his beautiful old language and your own at the same time, and it makes sense.

His eyes are deep tunnels of velvet blackness, and this is what you hear Him say: "These are my companions. Thank you for following them here. You have courage or else you would not have followed Dark Star all this way. Are you breathing?

"This Kingdom of Magic is still alive. It is called Avalon. No matter what anyone else might tell you, I have been here. It is more real than any world you have ever known. Look out from this window, and you'll see."

You look out the window. There is no glass...and there is the world. You can see that there are vertical ridges that shimmer with a silver green veneer, cracking like bark on a magic tree. In the depths of the ridges lie unknown, tall emanations of beauty. There are implications of trees, and you can feel leaves. Hollow, ancient vibrations knock on your heart, enabling you to see. All shapes are merely suggestive of forms familiar to your archaic memory. A feeling of vastness awakens in you.

As your eyesight rests upon this place, immediately a deep peaceful feeling begins to spread inside of you, and you know you are viewing the sublime realms. This causes your eyes to see differently.

"Come, and follow us, and we will enter the world together," (Jesus's voice).

As if in a parade you enter the line and follow these magic people out the door.

Air like this you have never seen or felt or smelled. Just breathing feels miraculous. Nothing is wrong. It seems not possible but there is a dragon here. Even though you are far away from it you can see every single scale, reflecting rainbows of light. Your eyes are telescopic now. Anything they land on, like the dew dropped spider web in the distance, is seen microscopically. Every droplet is shimmering with purple and green reflections.

All of those magic people sit down on the grass. They let you remain standing. There is the very faintest sound of music wafting through the air to your ears. Is it a flute, or a harp? It is indistinguishable, but you don't care, because you are not thinking. You are just purely experiencing.

There is the delicate, sweet smell of apple blossoms. This is the safest you have ever felt. It occurs to you to move your head and look around. There is the Lake, bordered by tall cattail reeds. It looks like there are castles moving under the water. And there is the Tor, with its circle of seven giant standing stones, reigning above all. You see the orchard of apple trees, for which Avalon is named, and each red apple is burnished with gold. Avalon is on a ley line, a dragon line, meaning that beneath it the Earth is a vortex of powerful magnetic currents. Beneath Avalon lies one of the most magical dragon lines on Earth.

Otherworldly peace hangs in the very air. You are not hungry, or thirsty. You have nothing to do. This sun shines upon you, warming your scalp in such a way you have never felt before. Combined with the smells, and the music, you feel lost in a dream.

But is it not the best dream you've ever had? It is not really a dream, because it is so real. A cat comes up to you, and meows. Or maybe it is a dog, barking. Just softly, enough to welcome you. There is Merlin, his purple robes dragging in the grass and his silver hair hanging about his face as he walks towards you with stars in his eyes. Merlin, the most famous of all magicians.

You've been admitted, just leave your mind at the door. Remember? It's in Chapter One. I told you, by reading this book, you become part of this dream. This is a spell. And you are here now. Thank you for following me. This belongs to all of us. Remember, I told you, only those with the magic bone can enter.

You feel Dark Star put her leopard paw on your shoulder. "Let it go," she purrs in your ear, and you can smell her. "Whatever it is, let it go."

"Do you want to be part of the beginning? This is the beginning of eternity."

You sit down against a stone, it looks like a tombstone, and sink into the lush moss of the earth. You breathe. Breathing in air is breathing in infinity. You accepted the invitation to come here, and become part of this. This is our masterpiece, and we share it together. Feel the peace and happiness, and pass it along. You can bring joy to others by sharing it.

I am the Axis, but you probably knew that. I who am Axis am not writing this to some broad group, but to you.

That is right, to You.

(Dark Star can still see your eyes reading).

You have joined this dream. You have joined this magic. You have come with me and walked this tightrope, the thread through time. Why not? I *knew* you had nothing to lose. You see, Avalon was *right here all along.*

Open your eyes and look out of them with your spirit. Open your mind and let down the drawbridge—because you *are the gateway.*

Avalon has risen up in us like a mountain, and has blossomed like the lotus flower.

EPILOGUE

Usually at the end of a book the epilogue is already known, and written.

In this case, *we* are the epilogue. As each human reads this, Avalon will become more tangible. That is the working of the spell. Because remember: There is one mind. There is one psyche.

Bringing Avalon back is something we all have to do *together*. It is a joint act; we all have to join forces; it's like the 100th monkey.

You have become part of the magic spell.

If you want to go to the place where Avalon is already coming back, go to the town of Glastonbury in Somerset, England and go to the Tor. Circle the Tor, and climb to the top of it. Can you smell between the worlds; smell the apple blossoms? *Because that is what happened to me.*

Thank you for taking part in the magic spell.

there is no end

DICTIONARY

This small dictionary reveals the meanings that are most close to the word's origin, and that are intended for the context of this book. The etymology is included where it is felt to be enlightening.

Avalon [*isle of apples*]: Isle of Avalon, district, originally an island, in SW England in Somerset including Glastonbury; an ancient school for the teaching of Druid magic (attacked in 563AD by Christian missionaries lead by "St." Columba); alleged burial place of King Arthur.

cryptic [from Greek kryptos *hidden*]: secret; hidden; mysterious; employing cipher or code; obscure.

dragon lines [aka ley line: the supposed line of a prehistoric track, with identifying points such as mounds marking its route]: underground lines of powerful magnetic current that meet and cross, making the land itself an easy access point into the otherworld; channels of electromagnetic energy.

druid [from Old Irish druid *magician*, Gaelic druidh *sorcerer*]: one of an ancient Celtic priesthood skilled in magical practices, natural sciences, and prophesy; bard, prophet. Druids were the doctors, scientists, lawyers and ministers to the Celtic tribes.

eerie: so mysterious, strange, or unexpected as to send a chill up the spine; seemingly not of earthly origin; exciting wonder or awe; extraordinary. syn *weird*.

lichen: a complex plant made up of an alga and a fungus growing in symbiotic association on a solid surface (as a rock or tree trunk); often appears as a pale green, flat, mosslike disk.

magic [from Greek magikos *of the Magi* (from Latin magi, plural, *members of a priestly caste*; also: *wise men from the east who came bearing gifts to the infant Jesus*, from Old Persian magus, *sorcerer*)]: natural and supernatural power or art seeming to have miraculous results; any mysterious, seemingly inexplicable, or extraordinary power or quality. syn *sorcery, alchemy, wizardry.*

megalith [from Greek mega *great,* lithos *stone*]: a rough stone of great size used as a monument or in construction of various types of prehistoric monuments (as Stonehenge).

Ogham [from Irish Ogma, *a mythical inventor of languages said to have invented the Ogham*]: a hidden way of writing, used by the ancient British and Irish, which provided signs for secret speech known only to the learned; was the sacred character of the Druids; also: an obscure mode of speaking used by the ancient Irish.

omen: an occurrence which anticipates a future event, good or evil; a prophetic sign, augury.

ominous: of the nature of an omen; serving to foretell the future; presaging events to come; portentous; eliciting amazement or wonder.

otherworldly: pertaining to a world other than that in which we actually live; relating to a world beyond death or beyond this reality.

pagan [from Latin paganus *country dweller*]: a follower of a polytheistic religion: one who believes in or worships more than one god.

parasamgate [Sanskrit]: the state of having gone beyond the beyond.

quicken, quickening [from Middle English quik, from Old English cwic; akin to Old Norse kvikr *living*]: to make alive, revive; to come to life; to shine more brightly. Quicken stresses a sudden renewal of life or activity especially in something inert. Archaic: kindle.

sarsen: a sandstone megalith used in prehistoric monuments and temples (as Stonehenge).

solemn [from Latin solemnis *festive*, from sollus *whole, entire*]: awe inspiring, sublime; performed with reverence, sacred; marked by grave sedateness and earnest sobriety.

soothe [from Old English sóð *truth*, Old High German sand *true*, Old Norse samr *true*, Gothic sunja *truth*, Greek eteos *true*, Sanskrit sant *being, existing, true, good, right*, Latin esse *to be*]: to prove or show to be true, verify; to offer relief or comfort to; to exert a soothing influence. Thus soothsayer: a speaker of truth or wisdom; a foreteller of future events.

trilithon [from Greek trilithos *of three stones*]: a prehistoric stone structure or monument consisting of two upright megaliths carrying a third as a lintel.

weird [from Old High German werd *worthy*, Old English wyrd, akin to Old Norse urthr *fate*, Old English weorthan *to become*]: n: the principle by which events are predetermined; fate, destiny; magical power, enchantment. adj: of extraordinary character; magical; fantastic; may imply unearthly or supernatural strangeness; mysterious. Also: an ancient British system of magic by the name of Wyrrd.

AUTHOR BIOGRAPHY

Lisa Lödy was born in upstate New York, and spent her childhood exploring her family's country property. Always in the woods, she fell in love with nature, collecting snake skins, feathers, and rocks while watching wild animals. Lisa graduated from Syracuse University, receiving a Bachelor of Arts degree in Psychology with a minor in English. She honed her craft by writing poetry. To prepare to write this book, Lisa conducted a twenty year long study of Native American and Druid shamanism. She traveled to the United Kingdom, investigating legendary sites, the most prominent being that after which this book is named, Avalon (the present Glastonbury in Somerset, England). Sage's cards Lisa designed and made herself; they helped write this book, and still exist today.

Lisa Lödy lives in Colorado.

CPSIA information can be obtained at www.ICGtesting.com
Printed in the USA
LVOW131325060713

341708LV00004B/742/P